GUN FEUD AT TIEDOWN

Price Jones reckoned the job as sheriff of Tiedown would be a cinch, seeing as how the worst trouble in years had been a ruckus with the Widow Henry over a toad in her bed.

But all of a sudden the country seemed to be busting wide open. There was a murder, a stickup, a stolen horse – and a race set up between the two cattle kings of the territory. Jones had the suspicion that these things were connected, that someone was stirring up this trouble, and he had until the day of the race to find out who.

GUN FEUD AT TIEDOWN

M

GUN FEUD AT TIEDOWN

by
Nelson Nye

MAGNA PRINT BOOKS
Long Preston, North Yorkshire,
England.

British Library Cataloguing in Publication Data

Nye, Nelson
  Gun feud at Tiedown.

  ISBN 1-85057-735-8

Printed and bound in Great Britain by
Redwood Press Limited   Melksham

Chapter One

LOOKING back you might be inclined to think most of the trouble had likely broken loose about the time the cow crowd – crocked to the gills that Saturday night, and more for the hell of it than anything else – proposed "Butterfly" Jones for high sheriff of Tiedown.

And you'd have been half right. The gamblers and chippies had gone along with the gag and the country's toughs had voted him in. There'd been a heap of back-slapping and considerable relief when the erstwhile law, sans shine of tin, had disappeared inside the southbound coach, which had promptly taken off like hell wouldn't have it.

The sleepy old town shook itself awake and took "a new lease on life," as they say in the papers. Money began to jingle and flow, new blood came in – the boom was on in feverish earnest, with street frontages selling at undreamed of prices and everyone flushed with this new excitement. It was a matter of indifference that two stages were stopped, Gattison's Print Shop wrecked, the Weekly Beller suspended. A ripple of talk made its rounds of the cow camps when the Purple Cow honky-tonk was taken for its cash at the point of a gun by three masked bandits.

But it wasn't until Harley Ferguson was found with pockets pulled out and his head caved in behind Bernagrowt's saddle shop some three weeks later, that a group of the town's more sober-minded citizens descended in a body on that prince of good fellows, the astonished Price Jones.

He'd been snoring it off in his grubby-looking underwear on the Army-surplus cot he'd moved into his office, a half-emptied bottle on the floor at his side. Disheveled and baffled, he sat up in his drawers to peer, bleary-eyed, at the indignant town fathers. "Wh-whasha matter?"

"Matter! Now see here," T. Ed Gretchen, the town's banker, said toothily, "you're holding this job under sufferance, you know!" And Eph Wilson, proprietor of Tiedown's largest mercantile store, declared with the look of a censorious beetle: "Either you straighten up quick and get down to business – the business you're drawing your stipend for – or you'll turn over that badge

10

to someone that kin!" And the rest of them nodded with self-righteous scowls.

Jones, with his jaw dropped open, blinked up at them stupidly. He fumbled a hand across unshaven cheeks and levered his ungainly length off the cot to stagger erect with an unstifled belch. "Whashat?"

It was hot in the office. The banker said, grimacing: "The man's impossible!" and patted his moist cheeks with a bit of crumpled linen. Growls rose from the others, and Flancher – who kept the town's only hotel – shook an irate finger under the new sheriff's nose. "By Gawd, Jones, we demand protection! You wanta go back to punchin' cows for a livin'?"

Jones grabbed up a bucket and reeled out to the pump. By the sounds of it, it hadn't been greased since Noah. He came back, still spluttering and dripping. With that scrawny mustache he looked more than ever like an underfed gopher, but at least he could move without stumbling into things.

His nose was too long, coming down like a beak over that ten-haired top lip. He made a gangling, slat-thin, shuffling shape, long-necked, bowlegged, oddly hunched through the shoulders as though the weight of that outsized lump in his neck was just about all

11

that a fellow could tote. As a cow nurse Jones had made a pretty fair hand, but cows weren't everything – even around here – and Flancher, eyeing him, was too disturbed to care a hang about tact. "You're a helluva lookin' specimen!"

The sheriff pawed sheepishly at his rumple of hair. "Guess," he said, "I must've tied on a beaut."

"What've you done about them stickups?"

"I'm workin' on them."

Five pairs of eyes stared back without favor. "If practice makes perfect," Bernagrowt began grumpily – but the hotel man cut in. "You got any idea what's been happening round here?"

Jones, peering about uneasily, mumbled: "Don't reckon you gents'd be so riled over nothin'."

"Nothing!" T. Ed Gretchen dragged his wilted handkerchief distractedly over his face again. "You're about as feeble an excuse for a peace officer as it's been my misfortune ever to come up against."

"An' we ain't goin' to stand fer it!" Bernagrowt tucked in, flapping his arms like a goonie stretching.

"Gentlemen – please!" Jones gulped with

both hands to his head. "If somebody'll tell me—"

"You hear about that card game in the Aces Up last night?"

Jones, with extreme caution, shook his head.

Wilson growled, "That minin' fella, Ferguson, come out high man. When the game broke up he had his pockets stuffed full—"

"An' turned up this mornin' with his head bashed in," Bernagrowt finished, "out back of my shop!"

"We want to know," the banker added, "what you propose to do about it. And your tenure in office as sheriff of this county will be determined – you might as well know this – by the results of your inquiry into Ferguson's brutal end!"

Having said this, T. Ed Gretchen put his handkerchief away, and, flanked by his satellites, irascibly departed.

Jones, groaning piteously, sagged to his cot and took his pounding head in both miserable hands. It was plain he was going to have to pull himself together, at least make a show of looking into that killing; but this wasn't a matter he felt up to tackling with his head whirling round like a chip in a millrace.

He floundered up, still groaning, and stomped into his boots. He got his hat, a cream-colored Stetson of the twelve-gallon variety, with a brim broad enough to keep the rain off his face – if any ever got to showing up in this country, where the oldest frog hadn't learned how to swim.

He stood there, frowning, with his mind on the drought and the cost of keeping horses in a desert where caterpillars and termites got the lion's share of what little grass infrequently came up. Then, his thoughts jumbling round again to Ferguson's misfortune, he fumbled into a blue-silk, go-to-hell shirt with red roses appliqued across the shoulders, and reached for the fawn-colored charro pants he'd got out of last night after caterwauling home from the Florencias' fandango. Glaring at the pants, he flung them down in disgust.

He'd thrown out all his work clothes when he'd quit his job at Rafter, not figuring to have any more use for them in the soft berth of sheriff in a place like Tiedown, whose greatest excitement in the past two terms had been the shrieks of the Widow Henry the time that horned toad had got into her bed.

14

Jones scowled longingly at his own. For two cents, by grab, he would've pounded his ear until his head felt more like tying into this business. He stood considering it seriously for a moment, then, with a shuddering sigh, he hauled his second-best pants from the tangled plunder wadded up in his warsack, and hopped around on one boot trying to pull the things on.

He was still clumsily trying, through a flow of abusive language, when a blocky, powerful bear of a man came shoving his forceful way through the door.

The guy came to a stand-still in scuffed, batwing chaps, pushing back the hat from his face the better to observe the sheriff's predicament. "Damn if you ain't a sight for sore eyes!" the big walloper said, cocking his head from one side to another. "Where the hell'd you dig up pants like them? Godey's Ladybook?"

Jones flushed with resentment. This was catalogue stuff he'd sent clean to Fort Worth for – the yellow boots alone had set him back two months' pay! "WHAT THE WELL-DRESSED CATTLEMAN WILL BE WEARING THIS FALL," was the heading on the page from which he'd made his selection. Let the dumb bastard laugh, he thought with disdain, and sank into a chair, thrusting out his bowlegs. "Catch hold of them boots, will you?"

Long Creek Trimbo wasn't pulling off boots for nobody. Looking down at Jones scornfully he blew out his cheeks. Planting both rope-scarred hands on his hips he began to swell up like a mule in a hailstorm, but the look of Jones was too much for him and he let his breath go in a snort of laughter. "The Great Seizer!" he hooted, then said derisively: "When you goin' to git onto yourself?"

Jones glowered, downright humiliated, putting on such a show before a dumb ox like Trimbo. He got the other boot into that dangling leg, and, though he dang near popped the seam in his anger, forced the stubborn boot through, and hauled the seat of the pants up over his butt. Fastening the front of them he caught up his shell belt, flung it about him, clinching it angrily. "This a slack stretch at your place?"

The man from Quarter Circle S took a hard, tighter look at him. "Waste of time, I reckon – told Geetch as much, but he was bound an' determined—"

"If this palaver's got a point how about shortcuttin' to it?"

Spangler's range boss said: "We had a horse hooked last night."

Jones, blinking, stared. "You pullin' my leg?"

"Any time I ride a dozen miles two ways through this kinda heat you better believe it ain't fer no joke. The horse was stolen. Geetch wants him back."

Price Jones looked like he didn't know yet if he was minded to swallow it. He'd heard some mighty mean things about Long Creek Trimbo and suspected that mostly they'd been told with restraint. Folks generally figured to give him plenty of room. Trimbo, maybe, didn't go out of his way to find a use for his talent, but the word had got around and no one who had sampled it wanted a second helping.

So now Jones said, as though feeling his way, "I ain't doubtin' your word, but you got to admit it don't sound a heap likely."

Trimbo grunted. "Crazier'n popcorn on a hot stove. If it had been Eight Below or Curtain Raiser even, a man might figure to make some sense of it. But the one that's gone is Papago Pete, a stove-up ol' geldin' no guy in his right mind would give fifty cents fer."

Jones scrubbed a hand across red-rimmed

eyes. "Maybe he just sort of wandered off."

"Didn't happen that way." Trimbo shook his head, scowling. "Some joker come right on into the yard, let down a couple bars an' cool as you please, put a hackamore on him, led him out to the road, hopped aboard an' took off."

Jones stared blankly. He couldn't see that it even began to make sense. And it made even less sense that a case-hardened bunch like Quarter Circle S would fetch a piddlin' deal like this to the law, when all of the years for as long as Price Jones had known anything about them, Spangler's outfit had run roughshod over anything and anyone that got in its way. Them and Grisswell's Gourd & Vine had just about, between them, run this country.

"The old man sick?"

"Geetch? Hell, no."

"So why come to me?"

"What I ast him myself, an' you know what he said?"

Jones shook his head.

"Said he didn't want to embarrass you. Said you was new to the job an' the least we could do was give you a chance to prove the voters hadn't made no mistake."

Jones peered suspiciously. "He never

18

brought nothin' to the law before."

"My very words," Trimbo nodded, cuffing the dust from his hat. "He explained that, too. Said times was changin' an' if it didn't discommode him he was willin' to change with 'em." The range boss grinned. "Get your nag an' let's go."

"Don't rush me," Jones flared. "Got all I can do right here for this morning. We had a killin' last night—"

"Could have another," Trimbo said mighty quiet, "if you an' me ain't arrived by the time Geetch gits there."

Chapter Two

DUST devils danced and the heat bore down as the sun climbed higher in a glare of sky and the wilted morning limped toward noon. Even the lizards had dug in out of sight, and the groaning Jones on the rack of his hangover bitterly wished he were dead a dozen times before they had been an hour on the road.

Heat lay over everything like a wriggling film, and off in the distance blue mountains shimmered as though shaped out of gelatin and tossed down still quivering. The sheriff closed burning eyes. His head felt tighter than a pounding drum but at least his stomach had finally quit churning, though he'd have felt a heap better if he could have downed his breakfast coffee. While saddling his horse he tried to pry a few facts out of Trimbo, but this had been about as helpful as hectoring a gatepost.

The country's vast silence began to get on his nerves. He still couldn't figure how he had got to be sheriff, but the badge on his shirt had opened a heap of doors he hadn't previously noticed, and in this new, enlarged view, the life he had come from had lost all its savor. Never had it looked so unpalatably bleak as it did right now, thinking back to that powwow he had just come away from. Them merchants was sure enough on the peck, and T. Ed Gretchen, besides being banker, was chief county commissioner – not the kind for talking just to hear his noggin rattle. He meant every dadgummed word of it!

Jones pried open his eyes to slant a covert look at Trimbo. The tough, beefy shine of that slab of a face did not encourage questions, but the banker's ultimatum finally drove Jones into voice.

"I want to know where you're takin' me."

Spangler's range boss, grunting, did not even look around.

Jones did not want any trouble with Trimbo but as sheriff he felt he deserved more than that. Grunts were for pigs and after stewing a while in squirming frustration he screwed up his courage for one more try. "I like to get along with folks," he said in a kind of scraped-up whine – "especially big taxpayers like your boss, Mr. Spangler, but . . ."

Trimbo, twisting one sardonic eye, said, "He'll be glad to know that," and relapsed into silence.

Jones considered a number of things it would please him to do, but all he actually put into motion was another nervous question. "No," Trimbo said, "I didn't see nobody."

"Then how do you know it was like you said? The horse *could* of—"

"I kin read, can't I?" Trimbo's frown stretched clear across both cheeks. "You debatin' my word?"

Looking into that flattening stare Jones, gulping, gasped for air and like a drowning man mumbled. "No . . . I'm just talkin'

. . . just trying to get at the facts."

Trimbo said with a sultry glower: "Any facts that's important you kin git from Geetch," and clamped his jaw like that was the end of it.

He was a hard man to like. Jones mopped his face with the back of a sleeve and thought nostalgically of his years on Rafter when all a man had to do for his wage was ride around after a bunch of cud-chewing cattle.

The sun, climbing higher, beat unmercifully down, and heat came off the ground in waves like a blast from the open door of an oven. Jones' eyeballs felt like they were starting to fry, and, somehow in his misery, he got to thinking about Trimbo's boss, the Number One man at this end of the cactus.

Though he had never swapped as much as two words with Geetch Spangler, he had seen him often enough in town, hellin' round with his crew or sitting in on a game at the Aces Up. It was common knowledge that Spangler had been here when Geronimo and his bronco Apaches had been riding and raiding all through this country.

Geetch had been the first stockman to settle in these parts and, by that token, had got the best range, adding to it from time to time other choice parcels which had taken his eye or dropped into his lap where others had found the going too rough. Nor had it yet been forgotten that where natural causes had proved less than sufficient to discourage some hardnose on land Spangler wanted, he had not been above plain-out driving them off.

It got to jouncing around through Jones' hammering skull that perhaps what had happened to Harley Ferguson out back of Bernagrowt's saddle shop last night might not be entirely unrelated to something Geetch wanted.

It was a soul-shaking thought, the kind to wriggle clear down into the very stones and mortar of a man's foundation.

The sheriff, shuddering, strove valiantly to disclaim it, and when this didn't help tried, copiously sweating, to push it into some far corner of his mind where he could go about his struggle to survive in relative comfort, reminding himself that in his mellowing old age, Spangler's chief concern and most present source of pride was the stable of short horses he had boastfully collected.

It was this reminder of Spangler's

23

sprinters that brought him round to pondering the region's other mogul, Grisswell, whose headquarters at Gourd & Vine was the county's finest show-place. And likely enough a thorn in Geetch's side.

No one – at least in Jones' hearing – had ever dared hint these two barons were rivals, but you could hardly mention one without including the other, and the pair, in this fashion, had been coupled so long out of deference, self-defense or for whatever reason, that anyone not wearing three-cornered pants must have sensed the general uneasiness progressively growing from such a situation.

Despite his fondness for strong drink and colorful garb, Butterfly Jones, though capable of much foolishness, was sharp enough in his own perverse fashion. He might never have got to the head of his class in the one-room schoolhouse he had briefly attended, but he had his allotted share of marbles and a certain native shrewdness or cunning, which, despite sundry fumbles, had kept him from foundering in the tides of adversity.

To put it bluntly, he hadn't made the scene for twenty-six years with his eyes plumb shut. He could see which side of the bread got the butter and now, adding up what little he knew and piecing out the bare bones with a couple of lively guesses, the notion he came up with was hard to abide.

Hollister Grisswell, with money he had made out of patent medicines, had bought into this country some five years back and proceeded to transform two rundown ranches and their hardscrabble holdings, via artesian wells and considerable irrigation, into about as lush a piece of landscape as could be readily found this side of the Rockies. He and his astonishing experiment made the accomplishments of Spangler look like pretty small potatoes, for despite Geetch's drive and bullypuss methods – not to mention half a life-time of grinding effort – his own headquarters out at Quarter Circle S, stacked beside Gourd & Vine, seemed more like a huddle of sharecropper shacks than home place of the country's first citizen. All Geetch's sweat had gone into expansion until he'd taken to this folly of collecting race horses. Summing up what he knew and tucking in what he suspected, the conviction Jones hit on was that something had to give – and here he was caught smack in the middle, sheriff of a county hunkered on a powder keg.

It was no dang wonder that tempers were short and Tiedown's town fathers felt so exposed they'd come swarming all over him. Another man in Jones' boots might have pitched in his star.

It would hardly be true to say the thought had not occurred to him. It had been all he could think of the last three or four miles but presently, groaning deep in his belly, he flung it aside. A little authority, if it doesn't plumb spoil him, can do wonders for a man and while, thus far, it hadn't done much for Jones, he was beyond all reasoning reluctant to give it up.

Trimbo, continuing dour and uncommunicative, never once pushed his horse beyond the animal's inclination, which was a sort of lazy shuffle. Heat lay across the dun horizon like smoke, the glare of sky pressed down with the weight of an iron fist. During the past several miles there'd been no sign of a road, but, suddenly coming onto one, Trimbo kneed his mount into it. Jones, eyeing him aghast, cried from an inward quaking: "Say – you gone off your rocker?" Peering ahead again he said, somewhat paler: "This here's the way to Gourd an' Vine!"

Trimbo, following his stare, said, "Damn

'fit ain't."

"What the devil we goin' out there for?"

"Orders was to fetch you. I don't ask Geetch for reasons."

Filled with inner turmoil Jones loosed a couple of gulps and – at least outwardly – subsided. Inside he was a mass of shaken jelly. No matter how he viewed it this trip looked like trouble, the kind of trouble that could get powerful bad and might easily dig someone a hole in short order. Maybe several someones – and it wasn't Geetch Spangler he was worried about.

Chapter Three

GRISSWELL'S place, when they presently came on it, was enough to squeeze any cowman's heart. It was like peering into the Promised Land, Jones thought, truly awed, as his eyes played over that broad sweep of valley, ringed by sugar-loaf hills turned the color of straw. Sunlit greens flecked with cool blue shadows, the stuccoed adobe great house and outbuildings trim and shipshape in a grove of cottonwoods, whose leafy branches waved and twinkled in a breeze alive with the intoxicating smell of this growing profusion of greenery.

Set down as it was in this drab country, with drought's sear hand laying over all else, it might have been taken for a bit of Kentucky snatched from the very heart of bluegrass, its lush meadows bounded by a crisscross of horse fence, the rails painted with loving care the same gleaming white that had been used on the buildings, the whole impression one of peace and plenty.

It just went to show, the sheriff told himself, what a feller could do if he had enough cash. The dude had brought in some white-faced bulls and the calves they saw – even the mother cows – made the kind of stuff Geetch Spangler ran look like the tag-end of nothing, which it was. Any one of those cows would have weighed three of Geetch's, and this grass was only part of the difference.

Trimbo, with his face tied in knots, growled from his wealth of brushpopper's scorn: "Them critters wouldn't last five days on the range!"

"Reckon you got somethin' there. Point is, though, they won't never have to. He's got more'n enough feed for them right on this

28

place. Bet he gets three cuttin's of that alfalfa! Prob'ly got his barns packed plumb to the roofs."

Trimbo flashed him an affronted stare, moved the cud in his cheek and copiously spat. "Let's git over there – there's Geetch now."

Following his look, Jones descried the Quarter Circle S owner putting his bay saddler down the horse-fenced lane which crossed the fields like a kind of levee in the direction of the distant tree-shaded headquarters. Reluctantly and with a cold lump forming someplace back of his navel the sheriff kneed his horse after Trimbo. He could think of forty places he would sooner be right now.

But there was no help for it. Trimbo plainly had the bit in his teeth and, while he made no effort to catch up with his boss, he moved right along, and the grip of his features in that gun-bore stare did not encourage Price Jones to hang back.

While they were still some distance short of the house and Spangler was stopping his horse by the steps, a chestnut-haired girl in what sure enough looked to be a man's pair of pants got up out of a chair and, bobbing a nod in the direction of Geetch, disappeared inside the house.

No one had to tell Jones this was Grisswell's daughter; the whole country knew she was home for the summer from that lah-de-dah girls' school she'd been going to at some frothy place they called Buzzard's Bay.

About the time Jones and Trimbo were reining up beside Spangler, who didn't bother to look around or even open his mouth, a portly white-haired geezer in a Palm Beach suit stepped out onto the porch with a welcoming smile. "A fine morning, gentlemen – very fine, indeed. I'm Hollister Grisswell. Come up and make yourselves comfortable. My daughter—"

"What I've got to say," Geetch broke in like he was Moses handing down the Ten Commandments, "can be said well enough right where I'm at."

He was a strapping six-footer, big, well-sprung, and lean with the gauntness of a timber wolf, which, with his yellow eyes, he more than a little resembled, Jones decided, especially the way his head with that ruff of dark hair was hunched forward, and with that glitter of teeth showing behind his peeled lips.

If Grisswell noticed this hostile glare it

was scarcely apparent in his courteous pause. "Don't doubt it a bit," he said with a chuckle, "but you'll find these chairs more roomy than a saddle, and my daughter will be along with some refreshments in a jiffy. Won't hurt you to stay long enough to have a drink."

"Didn't come fo' no drink," Spangler threw back gruffly, and the smile on Grisswell's mouth slipped a little. He had a tuft of hair on his chin like a goat, and Jones, chewing his lip, read real strength and considerable more savvy than was generally conceded in the fatty roll of those round and bland cheeks. Geetch, in his usual pile-driver fashion, drove roughshod on, contentiously declaring: "I didn't come over here t' chitchat with women!"

The mood of the man was plainly distrusting and cram-packed with belligerence.

"Well . . ." Grisswell said, "What *are* you here for?"

"We had a horse stole last night an' I mean t' find out what's become of him!"

Grisswell's widening look took in Jones and his badge and dark spots of color burned through his pale cheeks, yet he held himself in with remarkable restraint. "And you imagine he's here?"

"I'm goin' t' damn sure find out!"

The wicked arrogance of it pulled Grisswell's face out of shape, drained the last bit of color from his rigid cheeks. Jones, eyes goggling, hauled his jaw off his chest with an audible groan. Before the dude's resentment could leap out of him in words or he could lunge for a gun, the screen door flung open and the girl appeared with a tray of tall drinks.

She had put on a dress as red as spilled blood with a cameo brooch pulling it tight across her breasts, and with that freshly-brushed hair piled high above white temples, she would at any other moment have caught every eye, so regal, so lovely, was her obviously startled stance.

Jones, profusely sweating and aghast at his own temerity, cried into the breathless core of that hush: "You can't go through a man's property without due process – not, anyways, while *I'm* around!"

It fetched a flash of quick approval from the white-cheeked girl. The stupid, lost-lamb look of Grisswell's stare seemed even more bewildered in the wheel of baffled features; but what it drew from Spangler and his gun-hung hardcase was the cold, unwinking promise of dire action in the near future.

"We don't need no warrant," Geetch Spangler snapped and Grisswell fast recovering his aplomb, waved an airy arm. "Of course you don't," he declared with a dentifrice smile. "We have nothing to hide. Look anywhere you please."

Trimbo considered him with a darker stare as Geetch, reining away from the porch, sent his crow-hopping mount in the direction of the stables and the sprawl of pens beyond. Only Jones, half falling out of his saddle, seemed to feel the need to reach for a drink. Nor did he stand upon politeness in the matter. Snatching a frosted glass from the tray he threw back his head and with no thought but haste emptied it down the bobbing column of his throat.

Grimacing, he dragged a sleeve across his mouth and would have gone after the others had his glance not chanced to catch the girl's look. Her eyes were bright. She shyly smiled and Jones was caught like a fly in the world's oldest web. "It *is* hot, isn't it?" Cathie Grisswell said in the dulcet tones of Eve testing Adam, and her smile reached out to romp through him like a song.

It was the nearest Jones had ever been to

her and he sat transfixed, a startled grin on his face like a horticulturist caught up in the wonder of watching some delicate rare flower unfold. All else dropped out of his mind unmissed as the pull of this girl fastened onto his heartstrings.

Her father cleared his throat and swam into Jones' awareness. In the way of an appendage from some forgotten planet Grisswell's arm moved out to pick up a glass, but the spell lingered on until the medicine king's voice, suddenly leaping out of limbo, somewhat impatiently demanded: "What made him think, Sheriff, he would find the horse here?"

It took Jones a minute to break loose from his trance. Even when he found and finally placed the girl's father, he still looked pretty vague and kind of pawed at his face the way a man will trying to rid it of a spider web. "Ugh . . . what's that?"

"Why did the fellow think *I* had his horse?"

Butterfly hated to get back into that. "Search me," he frowned, trying to shrug it away. "Fact of the matter is I didn't even know what in Tophet we was here for till he come right out an' told you. It was Trimbo that come for me, an' you could sooner get

34

blood out of a rock than pry anything out of that mule-jawed jigger."

"Still," Grisswell said, as though turning it over, "he must have said *some*thing."

Jones shook his head. "You know as much as I do. All he told me was some guy waltzed into their yard last night, put a halter on this nag, led him out to the road, hopped aboard and took off."

Staring past Jones at some notion of his own, Cathie's father took a long pull from his glass. Pushing out his legs, fisting it, "Which horse was it?" he presently asked. "One of those two-twenty wonders he's so overbearingly proud of?"

"Nope," Jones said. "That's what's got him fightin' his hat. Accordin' to Trimbo it was that old geldin' they had been ponyin' 'em with. Trimbo swears the old skate wasn't even worth stable room – kept him outside in a pen. Sounds loco to – what's the matter?"

"A lead horse, you say?"

Grisswell cut the wrapped end from a pale green cigar with a tiny gold knife which he dropped on the table beside the tray the girl had put there, never taking his searching glance from Jones' face. His tongue rolled the weed from one end of his mouth to the other, and, when the sheriff nodded, he put a match to it, vigorously puffing until the swirls of blue smoke hemmed him in like fog.

From this haze his voice said like it was coated with honey: "County fair's coming up on the fifteenth, isn't it?"

Jones couldn't see any possible connection. "What's that got to do with the price of turnips?"

But Grisswell, waving the smoke away, smiled like a man who'd just come into an inheritance. "They'll be holding a race meet in connection with it, won't they?"

"Sure, but—"

"Open to the world?"

Jones, beginning to think this rich dude was even more loco than was generally supposed, stared uncomfortably, finally bobbing his head.

"There's nothing to prevent my entering a thoroughbred?"

"Not if you want to throw your money away."

"Money's only good for what a man can get out of it."

"You tie into them Steeldusts," Jones said disgustedly, "you won't get enough to buy one of them seegars!"

Grisswell smiled.

He sure was a dope. Cheeks flushed, Jones was minded to wash his hands of it, but a look at Cathie over there, plainly worried, made him say mighty earnest: "Mr. Grisswell, I'm tellin' you it would be plain murder. No thoroughbred yet has ever beat a short horse at the Tiedown county fair – why, these folks around here would go hog wild if you got into it."

"You think Mr. Spangler would make a little bet?"

Jones peered at him and gulped. "They'd take everything you got!"

Grisswell puffed contentedly, blowing out smoke rings like a steam locomotive. Maybe the dang fool *had* took that horse. If he figured to beat them top runners of Geetch's he didn't have enough sense to pound sand down a rat hole!

Chapter Four

JONES, with his initial disgust wearing off, had a pitying look wrapped across his cheeks when Spangler and his range boss, throwing hard looks at Grisswell, returned from the stables to sit their mounts in scowling silence.

The dude, Jones reckoned, was too dumb to be worried. Smiling benignly he said: "Now that you've seen for yourselves—"

"All we seen," Geetch snarled, "is that Pete ain't cached in none of them stalls. Don't prove you ain't got him – don't prove a damn thing!"

Grisswell, still in that patronizing tone, declared, "Really, gentlemen, this is pretty ridiculous. I wouldn't waste any time with that kind of horse, but if I *had* happened to want one I could have bought a whole carload and never missed the money. Whatever makes you think I would go out of my way to *steal* one?"

"Don't ask *me* why you done it," Geetch cried testily, rolling his eyes like a sore-back bull. He hauled in a deep breath and, glowering, growled: "If it's trouble you want—"

The dude flipped a hand. "I've heard what happened to some of your neighbors . . . burnings and beatings and broken bones. I'm not afraid of you, Spangler, and I don't intend to be pushed around. Do you understand that?"

Geetch looked like he had been kicked in the face, but more astonished than hurt. Then, abruptly, you could see his blood start to boil. His swollen eyes sank back into his head and he seemed in that moment to have entirely quit breathing. His yellow stare flattened out, turning silvery sharp as a two-pronged fork to reach out and slam Grisswell back against his chair.

In a terrible, half-strangled voice Spangler spoke. "We'll see who's afraid of who," he said, and his words had the slithery sound of a snake. "If that horse ain't put back powerful soon where he come from, somebody's goin' to pick up a skinned nose," and he slapped his mount on the rump, grabbing up his dropped reins.

Grisswell called: "Wait!" and Spangler's raw red cheeks came around. "Well?" he rasped.

Grisswell smiled with his teeth. "Understand you take an inordinate pride in that bunch of scrub broomtails you call running horses . . . even claiming, I hear, you've got the best stock there is. We've got a fair coming along in about ten days. There'll be racing, I suppose?"

"What about it?" Geetch said, truculent.

"I'd like to give this community a chance

39

to discover just how little you really are. I've got a horse I'll run against any nag you own—"

"Hoo hoo!" Geetch jeered. "That stolen pony horse, mebbe?"

"My stallion, Jubal Jo."

Spangler, head to one side, considered him, probably thinking back to the stock he and Trimbo had just looked through in Grisswell's stables. "Never heard of 'im," he scoffed.

The dude curled his lips. "You're hardly likely to have heard of a horse that has not raced. I'll tell you this much: he's by the Kentucky Derby winner, Plaudit, that defeated Lieber Karl."

"Humph. Thoroughbred, eh?"

"That's right."

"You poor deluded fool." Spangler looked his contempt. "You got no more chance'n a June frost at Yuma."

"Then why so reluctant?" Grisswell came back. "If you're so high on those short-winded dogs why not put your money where your mouth is?"

Spangler snorted. "You'd take on Curtain Raiser? Eight Below?"

"Makes no difference to me what you call them. Pick your best."

40

"How far?" Geetch said, beginning to show caution. "Half a mile?"

Grisswell laughed, saw it darken Geetch's cheeks. "What's your best distance? You're the challenged party. Make it easy on yourself."

Spangler and his range boss exchanged smug looks. "You hard-boot jaspers never learn a thing," Geetch declared, peering down at him, "but a man's a chump not to humor a sucker. If you're bound an' determined t' lose your shirt – an' you're still around come time for them races – I'll take you on for a quarter . . ." he was like a cat with some half-witted mouse – "for *five hundred a side!*" And he winked broadly at Trimbo, openly chuckling at the slick quick way he had snagged this dude on his own piece of twine.

The goddam peckerneck didn't know he was hooked.

Jones winced, embarrassed, as Grisswell in his most insufferable tone wanted to know if that was all Geetch could scrape up. "When I was talking to Gattison – our estimable printer – about the chances of getting out a broadside, the figure I thought of was ten thousand each."

Spangler's eyes boogered out like he'd

walked into a wall. The bright satisfaction fell completely away and he stared, mouth agape, unable to grasp this. Even Trimbo sat speechless.

"Those handbills are probably up by now, but of course," Grisswell said with a shake of the head, "if you're not that confident, or plain can't afford it, I suppose we can call the whole thing off. Seems a shame, in a way . . . everybody knowing . . . I suppose they'll figure I froze you out."

Spangler, cheeks livid, drew a shuddering breath and gasped. "Does it hev to all be *cash?*"

Grisswell appeared to mull this over, while everyone breathlessly hung on his words. "I don't think," he smiled, "I'd care to fool with notes, but if you want to put up that Hat Creek range with the buildings and equipment stored at Dead Soldier's Flat and throw in forty tons of top-quality hay in place of hard cash, you've got yourself a deal."

Geetch, as the dude laid down these terms, began to expand like a bad case of bloat. Crammed to the gills with insufferable emotions, the twisting fury raging through his blood seemed as threateningly explosive as a shook-up bottle of blasting oil, and Jones, peering nervously for something to get under, had the look of a man who thought the sky was going to fall.

Spangler couldn't speak he was so furious mad.

Grisswell wasn't done; he had to rub it in. "Sheriff," he said, "I call on you to bear me out. Spangler here, if I understand this right, undertakes on the second day of the Fair to run one of those puddingfoot crossbreds he named a moment ago – Eight Below or the one he calls Curtain Raiser – against my stallion Jubal Jo over a course of four hundred and forty measured yards. If he wins I pay him ten thousand dollars. If he loses he agrees to sign over to me forty tons of top quality hay, his Hat Creek range, plus the buildings and all equipment presently stored at Dead Soldier's Flat. Is that your understanding?"

Jones, not looking at Spangler, groaned, "Why don't you leave me out of this?"

The dude, sharply looking Jones up and down, said: "I would hate to believe, as the county's top officer, we've elected a man who's delinquent in his duty. You were here. You heard it. Is my summation correct?"

Jones lugubriously nodded.

Grisswell peered at Geetch. "Do you agree?"

Spangler glared like a dog with a bone. You could almost see the wheels going round.

He was convinced he would win unless his horse fell down. The logic of this was not open to argument – time and again Geetch had seen it proved. The tall, weedy thoroughbred, no matter how fast at bloodhorse distances, was a mighty poor risk against the short, chunky Steeldust in any all-out dash. It took most of those hardboots the biggest part of an eighth just to get up their steam, while the bred-for-it short horse reached maximum velocity inside three jumps.

The deal, as set up, gave Spangler all the advantages, and by that token it looked too good to be true. It was this that kept digging him. It didn't seem likely the dude could be such a chump. There had to be some kind of hanky-panky, some slick piece of trickery tucked away someplace. Nothing else made sense, and it worried him plenty. He stood to lose ten sections of the best graze he had.

The man's uneasy suspicions were plain

even to Jones.

"Well?" Grisswell spoke impatiently. "No one's forcing you, Spangler. You can still back down if you don't mind folks knowing—"

Geetch, beside himself, swore like a mule skinner. The dude had him over a barrel. He couldn't back down, not with everybody knowing it. He'd be laughed clean out of the goddam county! The look on the face of that stupid sheriff warned him how swiftly news of that sort would fly. He was a gaffed fish and knew it.

"All right," he snarled. "You're goin' t' know, by Gawd, you been in a horse race!"

Grisswell nodded. "There's just one more thing. Let's have it clearly understood that if for any reason this match is called off, or one of the horses fails to run when the time comes, the stake of the one who defaults is forfeit."

Geetch looked a long while and mighty hard at Grisswell before, with a grimace, he jerked his bitter face at Trimbo. "Let's git outa here," he grumbled.

Chapter Five

BUT just as they were wheeling and Jones – freed at last from his clutching dread – was shakenly reaching for a first dull breath, Spangler growled, twisting around to peer back across Trimbo, "You taken root there, Sheriff?"

The lump so prominent in Butterfly's neck popped up and down convulsively while he hung, bulge-eyed, like a fish out of water. His chin sort of trembled like the lip of a stove-up horse, but nothing came out that a man could hear or see.

It was Cathie who cried brightly, "But he can't go *now!* He promised to stay for lunch and it's practically on the table!"

And her father fondly said, pushing up with his rich man's smile, "You'll find a promise to Cathie about as easy to wriggle out of as a straitjacket, my boy. And you did promise – remember?"

Jones, finding his voice, gulped. "Dang if I didn't," and, dropping his reins, commenced to flounder toward the porch.

Through sweat-soaked shirt he could feel the burn of Spangler's stare. Any moment the man, always unpredictable, might do something drastic, and even though he didn't Jones, with dry throat, had a frightening hunch he had not heard the last of this. But he went doggedly on after the girl's lissome figure, trailing her through the pulled-open screen and into the cool and ornate security of the medicine king's home.

Through the myriad wonders of a shuttered withdrawing room, Cathie led him to an elegant horsehair sofa and, seating herself beside him – at a properly virtuous distance of course – said through the shine of a tremulous smile, "I don't know what you must think of me, telling such a fib. You didn't really *want* to go back with them, did you?"

The gist of her rhetorical question entirely escaped him – all he heard was the tinkle of her mission-bell voice, soothing and soft as the wings of young doves. He felt queerly light-headed staring into her eyes, permeated with the dizzy sort of wonder that overtakes converts on their pilgrimage to Mecca. Perhaps he had been in the sun too long. He gulped and stammered, foolishly grinning. She was thrilled, he could see, just to be in his company, even crossing her legs to lean a little closer.

"I think sheriffs," she said, peering up into his face, "must be terribly brave. I

47

almost swooned when you stood up to that horrible Geetch Spangler, daring him to search our ranch without a warrant – but I was proud of you, too. Imagine him thinking we would take his old nag! As though Daddy would have any use for it. Ugh!"

It did sound loco but Jones, recollecting, fought up out of his trance to say, "Accordin' to Trimbo—"

"That man's got rocks in his head!"

"Umm . . . well, there ain't nothin' wrong with his eyes that I've noticed. He claims the tracks headed straight for this ranch."

"Claims! Did *you* see any tracks?"

"No, but—"

"Of course you didn't or anyone else. The whole thing's preposterous! I think Daddy's right," she cried, flapping her eyes at him. "I think Spangler wants to take over this ranch; he resents Daddy bitterly – he can't stand the thought of someone else being important. Look what he did to the rest of his neighbors – I've heard the stories!" Her eyes took hold of him. "Have you killed many people?" she asked low and breathless.

"Well – no," Jones confessed, swallowing

uncomfortably.

But her look said she knew he was just being modest. "I've heard about Masterson and Mossman, all those others. A man has to have a great deal of experience, my father says, nerves of steel and be a dead shot before he can hope to be elected sheriff." She considered him intensely. "Would you do something for me?"

Jones, badly rattled, stared aghast. "You – you mean – *kill* somebody?"

"Silly! Please be serious," she said, gripping his arm. "I want you to write in my autograph album; I'm collecting signatures of famous people."

Batting those pansy eyes at him again, "I want *yours*," she cried prettily, jumping up to hang over him. The hand she extended was warm, firm, and astonishingly urgent. There was a fragrance about her reminiscent of crushed violets, and something indescribably exciting left its bright track across the turn of her glance. In that bent-forward face her enormous eyes looked weirdly blue-purple. Jones was briefly reminded of Concord grapes; then she tugged at him harder. "It's in my room – come on!" she impatiently whispered.

Tipped toward him like that he got to see

more of Cathie than was generally discernible. His cheeks turned hot, his head pounded fiercely, yet he was not without a rather horrid sort of anticipatory tingle as he allowed her to pull him to his feet.

He wasn't rightly sure just what she had in mind, but despite his jumbled notions he was immensely relieved when, before she could snake him into deeper water, a frozen-faced butler arrived to announce lunch.

Jones stumbled after him, copiously sweating.

Back in town some three hours later, having cared for his horse, Tiedown's new sheriff – tired, disgruntled, and about as uneasy in the churn of his thoughts as a one-legged paper hanger fresh out of stickum – stepped into the trapped heat of his two-by-four office to find it filled with the shapes of waiting men.

He didn't care for the way they looked at him, and when Bud Flancher growled, "Where the hell you been?" Jones knocked the top off his can of private cusswords. "I been busy," he flared, "tryin' to find a stolen horse – an' if you got to know more you better jump on your bronc an' lope out for a gab with the brass-collar dog of these here localities! The mogul who figures he pays most of my salary an' expects me t' leap through hoops when he whistles!"

The hotel man edged back with his mouth flapping, and a kind of frozen hush seemed to grip the whole push except T. Ed Gretchen who, being town banker with a safe full of plasters, considered himself immune to the disasters which frequently haunted his less affluent depositors.

"You've been to Quarter Circle S?"

"I've been to Gourd and Vine, too – an' what's been happenin' round this burg don't hold a patch to the trouble that's buildin' between Spangler an' Grisswell. Here," Jones growled, thrusting a torn and badly wrinkled broadsheet under the banker's quivering nose – "read that! An' if that ain't enough, grab hold of your hat. Geetch has practically accused that confounded dude of stealin' the horse Trimbo says was made off with!"

Shocked gasps met this news; but Gretchen, never looking at the paper Jones had passed him, said above the panicked groans: "I believe the county seat has first call on the professed abilities for which you were elected. The commissioners when they visited you this morning handed down an ultimatum. What have you done about it?"

Jones said sullenly: "How many legs you think I got?"

"Results is what we're interested in. We want to know what you've done about Ferguson's—"

"Who's Harley Ferguson," Jones demanded, "that every clock should stop because—"

Gretchen said with vast patience: "Just a two-bit leaser trying to make a winning from a played-out hole. It's not *who* he was we're concerned about but *what happened to him* and *where*. You go off all day tearing around after some horse while murder stalks the streets of—"

"We ain't goin' t' stand for it!" Flancher broke in, furious. "It's a matter of public safety!" he cried. "Not a one of us is safe – man, woman or child, while some loco killer—"

"I can't be more than one place at one time!"

"What we're trying' to pound through your stupid head," Eph Wilson, the Mercantile's owner, snarled, "is, your place is *here!* Us merchants are paying for police protection."

"Yeh," mimicked Jones, "two cents on the dollar! That'll buy enough for about three snorts!"

Eyeing them scathingly he said, fed up: "I got no reason to speak up for Geetch Spangler, but year in an' year out he pays more taxes than all you counter-jumpers piled in one heap. He's got a *right* to expect some return, by grab. Here – take your damn tin," he cried, ripping off his badge. "Shove it up your you-know-what!"

They peered, drop-jawed, incredulous and aghast, eyes looking like they would flop off their cheekbones. "B – but you *can't* do that . . ." the banker gasped, jowls quivering. "You swore to uphold—"

"I didn't know then what a cheapjack bunch of fritterin' old women was goin' to be hangin' over me all the time. An' I never give out t' buck up ag'in *murder!*"

"You reckon we pay out eighty a month for you to set on your pratt and buck Old Crow?" Flancher looked for two cents like he'd take hold of Jones.

But, somewhere among the dark crosses of office and frightening glimpses of things to come, Price Jones' spinal column must have picked up some starch. "There's your badge," he cried – "put it on, why don't-cha, an' see how far *you* git!"

In the hush that reached out while he

paused to grab breath, the rest of them stood like they were hacked out of wood, and damned poor wood at that.

He showed his scorn in a jeering grin. "Someone around here is goin' to have to face up to what's about t' come down on you. Take a squint at that paper Gretchen's wavin' around. You beller about what happened to that leaser. One stiff ain't *nothin'*; git your eyes open, man! You're liable, before this is done, t' have 'em stacked in the alleys three an' four deep."

Grabbing the paper the burly saloonman spread it out. "Cripes amighty! Account of a *horse race?*" he said in disgust.

"Account of what it can lead to when one of 'em gits beat. You don't see it?" Jones stared. "Spangler an' Grisswell. Biggest men in this county. How many, you reckon, can stay outa this when them two gits on the prod for sure? The feud they're hatchin' can split this county end for end; it sure won't be no place for women an' kids then."

Eph Wilson and Gretchen turned dubious, nervous; even Flancher began to show signs of worry. Bernagrowt anxiously eyed the banker. "He just might be right. Remember how it was that time Geetch took after them Collison brothers . . ."

54

And the storekeeper said in his E-string whine, "Maybe, if we was to raise him twenty dollars, Butterfly here could be persuaded to stay on—"

Jones, glowering, said: "Do I look like a *fool?* You think twenty bucks would make up for gettin' planted?"

Flancher growled: "You was willin' enough when there wasn't no trouble. What the hell are you, a man or a mouse?"

Jones didn't like what he saw on their faces. He didn't like any part of this. But if he quit on the job now the whole country would figure he'd been scared off – he could see it in their eyes. *No*body would hire him, not around here. "Well . . ." he said, wavering, and T. Ed Gretchen stepped into the breach.

"Tell you what we'll do," he said, and pinned the star back on Butterfly's shirt. "We'll up you another twenty a month and give you a deputy. That's fair enough, isn't it, to keep on with a job you've already sworn to do?"

Jones, far from sure, edgily nibbled his lip. He considered the advantages. "All right," he grumbled, "but no more delegations. I want it understood I'm to have a free hand."

Chapter Six

TROUBLE was, he figured out later, a man – hating to be set up for any kind of patsy – dislikes even more to seem an out-and-out coward.

But nothing had changed. No part of the ruckus he had sensed shaping up appeared any less touchy on sober reflection. Sure, he'd been upped twenty bucks a month to stay with it – drawing now the equivalent of a foreman's wage – plus the further concession of a deputy to work off his frustrations on; but he was still uncomfortably nagged by the suspicion Ed Gretchen and them others had someway jobbed him.

He went out for his supper and when he got back the office lamp had been lighted. Through the dust clinging thick to the cobwebby window he could see someone hunched over the desk with a pencil.

More grief, he reckoned, yanking open the sagging screen; and stopped dead upon discovering it was the county coroner. "Well, fan my saddle! Ain't you kinda premachoor?"

The man at the desk brushed a hand across his jaw. Eyes that were almost black came up, peering at Jones and plainly not seeing him.

"I ain't dead *yet*," Butterfly snorted. Harold Terrazas had always made Jones a little uncomfortable. On top of everything else he found it hard to understand how any man with real bone in his spinal column could be content to be doodling around with a pencil all the time. Some of the animals he drew looked likely enough to get right up and walk off the paper. You had to give him that.

Jones grumbled: "You hear about me gittin' a raise?" and pushed out his chest, dragging a sleeve across the shine of his star before going over to flop on his cot. "Just let 'em know if they figured to keep me, they had to git off my back an' sweeten the pot. Them fellers ain't dumb," he told the Mexican, nodding. "They could see plain enough—"

"Yeah. Twenty dollars worth. You sure hung it on them."

Something about the way that was said yanked a closer look from the long arm of the law. "That wasn't all they give me," Jones grumbled, bristling. He couldn't think why he should defend himself but that melancholy stare brought back all his doubts. He cried, almost snarling: "They even throwed in a deputy!"

"I know. Me." Terrazas sighed.

Jones, feeling better, had got as far as reaching for a vindicated breath before the jolt in those words caught up with him. "You!"

For a moment there, flapping up off that cot, you might have reckoned he had picked up a coral snake. He had that waxen look that sometimes grabs onto faces at the reading of a will.

"But they can't do that!" he cried.

"What I told them. They done it anyhow."

"But you're the coroner, man!"

"My very words. You know what that sonvabitch banker said? Said they was giving me the chance to work out my 'indebtedness' – like it was *my* fault no one ever dies around here! There isn't a grateful bone in that bugger's whole body." He heaved a shuddering sigh.

And then remembering, "Even had to buy me a gun, and all they'll put up toward transportation is the shoe bills and grain cost, and not even that unless I'm out on the road."

His well-padded frame quivered, like

jelly. "Chihuahua!" he groaned, then looked up to say, thoughtfully, "You're wrong about Spangler."

Jones' chin kind of set after the way of a stubborn mule, and a bad look came out of him. "What d'ya mean, wrong?"

"I don't think he's— Why would he want to be kicking up trouble?"

"Why does a hen cross a road?" the sheriff scowled. "It's his nature, that's why. When you've put up with the kind of things I cut my teeth on—"

"I know the guy's pushy. Gritty as fish eggs rolled in sand – and *proud!* I'll give you that, but he's in mighty poor flesh to be courting ambition. He's had three bad years, and this drought—"

"He don't worry about drought! Why should he? He's got every waterhole sewed up—"

"And most of them so dry you couldn't make mud if you spit all day." Terrazas appeared to have given much thought to this, and said now earnestly: "He's got no patent to the Verdigris River and Grisswell's straddled smack above him, both sides. You ever think about that?"

Jones snorting, said, "All he's ever *done* is make trouble! You can't git around that!

An' Trimbo . . . what you reckon . . ."

"Trimbo could be part of it, maybe," the coroner conceded with an unsure frown, "but there's more to this than Trimbo." He considered Jones darkly. "You must have heard he's been losing beef?"

"Nothin' to it," Butterfly scoffed. "You're talkin' about that hill crowd west of him. If there was anythin' in it he'd of clumb all over 'em." Jones looked his disgust. "You think he'd hold still for a thing like that!"

"Don't guess he could help himself."

"That'll be the day! Any time that ol' wolf—"

"He's an old man, Price. Half his crew's quit." Terrazas leaned forward earnestly and, with Jones saturninely eyeing him, said: "It's the truth. Six of his hands pulled out on today's noon stage; whole town's been talking."

"Musta been fired then. Man don't quit when he's hired out to Spangler. Not without . . . The noon stage, eh? They musta sneaked off while him an'—"

"Flip Farley claimed there haven't any of them been paid in the past four months. Geetch has been passing out I.O.U's. You can ask Ed Gretchen – he was standing right

60

there."

Jones stared with his mouth open.

"Geetch must be in a pretty bad way – for cash, anyhow," Terrazas said, straightening. "And this wager . . ." He got out one of the broadsheets Gattison had printed. "You think if he could get hold of cash he'd have put up that Hat Creek range of his? Who started this race talk anyway – him?"

"Well, no," Jones admitted.

"And here's something else. I went around to the Aces Up after those boys left and had a talk with the barkeep. It's true, right enough. Spangler's crew has been passing Geetch's paper. Barkeep said his boss had put a stop to it, and I got the same story at the Purple Cow." He peered at Jones darkly.

Jones tugged his mustache, looking beat and worried.

"Like you," Terrazas said, "I think we're in for a squall. I can't help feeling someone's *nursing* this feud, but I don't believe it's Geetch. I think it's someone outside who's got his plans laid for a killing. Someone," he said grimly, "who knows the spot Spangler's in and not only where to jab him but—"

Boots crossed the stoop with an urgent

ching of rowels. The screen was yanked open and disclosed the excited lamplit face of Shores, Grisswell's ranch manager. Ignoring Terrazas, Shores cried at Jones: "You better get out to Gourd and Vine, Sheriff – someone out there is trying to kill Mr. Grisswell!"

Chapter Seven

JONES gaped like someone who'd been poked in the stomach. Grisswell's man, swinging around, pinned Terrazas with an exasperated stare. "Can't he hear? What's the matter with him?"

The coroner, with Latin eloquence, shrugged.

"Hell," Butterfly growled, abruptly coming to life. "When'd it happen? Who done it? Is the old fool dead?"

Shores' eyes bulged like grapes beneath the snapbrim hat. "He . . . ah . . . wasn't when I left . . ." Florid cheeks mottling to a fish-belly white, he said in a half-strangled outrage: "I'll thank you, my good man, to employ a civil tongue. Mr. Hollister

Grisswell is a person of considerable substance, a pharmaceutical wizard, a—"

"I didn't ask for a pedigree."

"My dear fellow," Shores said, "we're discussing a Ghengis Khan of the financial world who cannot be dismissed with a wave of the hand. As a man of vast interests, one of your largest taxpayers and most influential—"

Jones made a vulgar noise with his mouth and the other man, shocked, drew himself to his full height. Looking down his nose he declaimed with umbrage: "I would advise . . ." and, faltering, backed off as Jones came toward him like a runaway freight, fists doubled, jaws grinding audibly.

"Now you listen to me! All I been gittin' all day is advice! I don't want any more so choke off the blat! I left your place at two. Then what happened?"

Eldon Shores in his scissorsbill hat and tweedy plus fours had been fetched West from Chicago. He was scoffingly referred to around Tiedown as a "buggy boss," as foreign to this element as a cow is to bloomers. He was a man from the world of papers and figures. Appalled by the crudeness of his present surroundings, his defense was contempt, the arrogance of patronage. But faced with the cantankerous look of Price Jones this facade began to crumble.

Shaken, he said: "I don't know. I was in my office going over the books. I – I'm afraid I rather lost track of time. I heard a shot. It seemed to come from outside. As I ran into the yard there was a second shot, the kind of flat crack you get from a rifle, then a thudding of hoofs beyond the big barn."

He swallowed nervously. "I dashed into the stables. Miss Cathie appeared in the door of the pens. "It's Daddy!" she said. "Someone's trying to kill him! Oh – hurry!' she cried, and I dashed toward the—"

"Was he hit?"

"Well . . . no," Shores replied with an irascible look, "but one of our horses—"

"Then all you're doin' is guessin'," Jones said. "Sounds a heap more like somebody was tryin' to throw a fright into him."

"Mr. Grisswell isn't easily frightened."

"He honestly thinks this jigger tried to—?"

"I suggest you talk to Mr. Grisswell himself. He said something about the Lord apparently having more work for him; it was a mighty near thing. One of those bullets tore the sleeve of his shirt. The other nicked his left ear—"

"I thought you said he wasn't hit!"

"It looked more a burn than a hit, hardly broke the skin. But," Shores cried indignantly, "if it had struck any closer it would have torn off his jaw!"

Butterfly, grunting, scooped up his hat. "Mind the store," he told Terrazas.

Grisswell's ranch manager, starting to put out a hand and then – considering Jones' look – deciding against it, said "Where are you off to?" But the sheriff, jaws clamped, shoved open the door and, without bothering to answer, departed.

By the wash of the stars it was nearing ten o'clock when he picked up the lights of Gourd & Vine. Tired and irritable, it came over him now he had probably put in this ride for nothing. He could stay over, of course, and have a look in the morning. If it wasn't so late he could have chinned with the girl – not that the prospect was unadulterated joy, still you had to admit she'd gone out of her way . . . Jones, groaning, rode on to pull up by the porch. She was the only millionaire's daughter he had ever been close to, and she was sure some different than he had figured she'd be.

Just thinking about her put him in a cold sweat.

The bunkhouse was dark. All the lights he had seen appeared to come from the house. He sat there a moment then called, "Anybody home?"

He heard steps and then Cathie's form was pressed against the lamp-lit screen. Her lifted hands closed round her face and for a couple of seconds she stood wholly still, peering. "Who – who is it?" she called in a thin, frightened voice.

Butterfly gulped. "Price Jones," he said, and she flung open the screen to hurry prettily out and stop at the top of the steps, widely staring, while Jones' pounding heart threatened to burst from his chest.

"Is it really you?" And when he said that it was, and got out of the saddle, she ran down the steps to bury her face against his chest. He could feel her shake through the moan of her sobs. Over her head Price Jones scowled fiercely. "There, there," he grumbled, clumsily patting her.

"I thought you *never* would come!" she wailed. But she got hold of herself quick enough when he said, "You know? I been thinkin'. Be a fine how-de-do an' six hands around if someone from this place – that prissy-mouthed Shores or some other hired hand – actually did lift Geetch's horse."

She pulled back from him, stiff as a touched gopher. "Are you out of your mind!"

The stab of her eyes was like polished glass, then a bark of a laugh tumbled out of her and she straightened, hands poking her hair, to say ruefully, "I declare you had me going for a moment. Where *is* Mr. Shores – he hasn't been hurt, has he?"

"He'll be along, I expect. I'd like to talk to your father."

"You'll have to wait till tomorrow then. I gave him a hot toddy and put him to bed. Poor lamb, this thing really took it out of him . . . the shock, and all. He looked awful; but I can show you the place if you have to get back. The tracks, I mean."

Jones rubbed his jaw. She looked at him brightly. "We'd be glad to have you stay; there's plenty of room in the bunkhouse. We don't keep a big crew. A place like this, irrigated and fenced . . . just a matter of rotation; about all the hands have to do is push levers."

"You know where the shots were fired from?"

"That little hill with the hackberries just

above the pens."

"Well . . . if it wouldn't be too much bother?"

"No bother at all. Come on," she said, reaching out for his hand.

She found a lantern in the barn and when Jones put a match to it several of the kept-up horses softly nickered and one, a big black, restively pawed for attention. "That's Jubal," she laughed. "I'm afraid he's spoiled rotten."

Jones followed her through a far door that opened onto the corrals. "Did Eldon tell you one of our horses was killed? One of our bred mares in foal to Jubal Jo," Cathie said. "She'd been having some trouble. That's why Daddy was out here. And this is where they were," she said, pointing, "in that corner there by the tank."

Butterfly held up the lantern. "What happened to the mare?"

"She's dead." Cathie shuddered. "One of those bullets that were meant for Daddy—"

"I mean, where is she now?"

"Oh. Eldon had the crew bury her. This heat . . ."

"All right." Jones couldn't see that it made much difference; he couldn't learn anything from eyeing a dead horse. "Let's git up on that hill." He did think, though, they might have waited till he saw it.

He said, walking beside her, "You have much trouble finding—?"

"Not too much. One of the hands saw the fellow when he was trying to get away."

"*Saw* him?" Jones stopped.

"Not really. Just a glimpse as the man went tearing off through the brush – over beyond our south fence, you know."

Jones eyed her sharply. "Toward Spangler's Hat Creek range?"

"Well, yes, I suppose so . . . if that's what's south of us. I don't really know. I've been so upset about Daddy—"

"Anyone pick up his sign?"

"The boy that caught that glimpse of him tried. He left a pretty plain trail till he climbed from the wash. When the tracks ran out in that lava spill Joe followed them back up here to this hill, which is how we discovered where the shots had come from."

Puffing a little from the exertion of the climb they moved into the trees. This was more a clump than any real kind of woods, scarcely shoulder high, a tiny jungle of canes topped by splotches of foliage. Jones, boring deeper, holding up the lantern, picked out the drygulcher's nest from a trail of broken branches. He found three cigarette stubs, hand-rolled, and one ejected cartridge case, but the ground was too hard for any useful prints.

Pocketing the shell he shoved on through with his eyes peeled for horse tracks. He found tracks, two sets, so inextricably mixed not even a Chinese lawyer would have been able to unravel them. He would have liked to have booted that Joe clean to Halifax. But swearing wasn't going to help him any.

Rejoining the girl he told her grumpily, "That hand of yours that went to look at them tracks did everything but roll in 'em."

She said defensively, "He was just trying to help—"

"He helped, all right. We might as well go back. There ain't nothing here."

On the way to the house he remained uncommonly silent. At the porch about to swing up, he said gruffly, "You want I should send the doc out t' look at him?"

"At Daddy?" He thought she sounded sort of astonished. Then she said, darkly sober, "He isn't going to like it, but maybe it *would* be a good idea. If he'll come out in the morning . . ."

"I'll send him," Jones grunted, and went into the saddle. "I'm obliged for your help." He lifted his hat and put the horse into motion, somehow glad she hadn't seen him pick up that shell.

He twisted around once in the drive to find her watching just where he'd left her. Seeing her lift a hesitant hand, Jones waved back, prickled with goose bumps. Then, remembering that shell, he cursed under his breath.

The tinny sound of an off-key piano tinkled up from the street while he stabled his mount. Bone-weary, disgusted, bad in need of a drink, Jones was strongly minded to go tie one on. Instead, he went dragging his spurs down the echoing planks, glumly bound for the jail, dismally filled with the look of a town he had never seen soberly before at 3 a.m.

The office, though dark, was neither empty nor quiet. Snores filtered raucously through the baggy, patched screen, and he pulled up, to sourly peer once again toward the Purple Cow before, grunting, he yanked open the squeaking door and let it bang.

A series of spluttering snorts came from the cot and a shape pushed darkly up and grew still behind the metallic rasp of a cocked six-shooter. "Oh, fer cripes sake," Jones growled testily, "light the lamp."

In the yellow glow Terrazas scratched himself and pushed an irritable hand through his disheveled hair. "Did you have to get me up in the middle of the night?"

Jones, saying nothing, set the cartridge case down on the desk beside the lamp. Terrazas in his long-handled drawers bent nearer. His eyes came up sharply. "That dude ain't dead is he?"

Butterfly, irascibly shaking his head, said, "Look at that damn thing!"

Terrazas curiously picked the shell up, turning it about in his competent fingers. "Buffalo gun. What's the matter with it?"

"Well," Jones said, "it come from where that dry-gulcher stood. Fired from a rifle chambered for the .45-120-550 – a *Sharps*! You know anybody around here besides Geetch that's got one?"

Chapter Eight

DURING the weeks that followed Jones got nowhere at all. For all he and Terrazas accomplished they might as well have been out punching cows. Separately and sometimes together the sheriff and Terrazas conversed with a gamut of people, but nothing they discovered appeared to advance their investigations by one substantial fact. They failed to unearth a single lead which might disclose the identities of the three masked rowdies who had stuck up the Purple Cow. They got nowhere with the killing of Harley Ferguson, and the more they cudgeled their brains about Spangler the blacker he looked.

After quitting Gourd & Vine the day Jones had stayed on for lunch, Geetch could have easily turned back, or sent Long Creek Trimbo to trigger the pair of slugs which had dropped Grisswell's mare. Terrazas took the view that, whoever it was, all they'd really intended was to throw a good fright into Grisswell; but Jones, though he nodded, was a long way from sure.

Both Geetch and Trimbo had sat in on that Aces Up poker game which had put such a tempting load in Ferguson's pockets. Butterfly had not questioned either man, not wanting, he told Terrazas, to tip his hand. But the coroner, sounding out others, discovered it to be the general opinion that once the game had broken up, the pair from Quarter Circle S had left straightaway for the stable to get their horses and take off.

Actually, it appeared, they had left the saloon some fifteen minutes ahead of the leaser.

Just for the hell of it Jones had dropped around to shoot the breeze with the liveryman, and almost gave himself away when he was told: "No Spangler horses was here. The night you're talkin' about that Quarter Circle S bunch had their broncs all tied along the street. In front of Bernagrowt's shop, I think it was."

Considerably exercised, Butterfly had Terrazas talk to the Dutchman. Yes, the saddlemaker said, six or seven Spangler-branded mounts had been racked before his place. He couldn't say how long they'd remained there but they were still out front when he'd gone home at eight o'clock.

Jones went around to have a look at the hotel guest book. Flancher himself was on duty and, at the sheriff's request, pushed it over for Jones to leaf through. Flancher was nobody's fool. Lowering his voice he said, eyeing the date, "If it's Geetch you're figuring to look up, he was here."

Jones flattened his lips. "All night?"

"As to that I couldn't say. The bed was used. That's all I can tell you. I didn't see him come in. I didn't see him leave."

Jones, enjoining silence, thanked the man for his help and, like a kid going barefoot across sun-blistered tarmacadam, took a somewhat abrupt and gingerly departure. Flancher may have spoken straight from gospel, but Spangler's name had not been on that page.

Though they worried it like two dogs with a bone, neither the sheriff nor his deputy could turn up one soul who would admit to having seen Harley Ferguson alive after leaving the Aces Up. About the only unswervable thing they pinned down was that Geetch had been playing with paper in the game and had "sure dropped a bundle."

They fooled around for a while with the reasonable theory that the theft of Spangler's horse, the Purple Cow holdup and Ferguson's murder might be wholly unrelated rather than stemming from a single mind, but this proved too much for Jones to swallow.

"You're probably right," Terrazas reluctantly grumbled, holding off to scan through half-shut lids the sketch he'd just made of the disgruntled sheriff. "Besides," he said, sighing, "it doesn't take into account what happened to Gattison."

"Oh, my gosh!" Jones exploded. "You

reckon that's part of it?"

The coroner tossed aside his handiwork. "We'd be stupid to overlook it. Putting that print shop out of commission probably kicked off this crime wave." He frowned. "A logical opener. It put the paper out of business. And it's the kind of thing Geetch would do."

Butterfly shoved baffled hands through his hair. "He's violent enough to of done it. But somehow I never did figure him for smart. A feller that would throw all he has into horses—"

"He's like an old cranky wolf with one foot in a trap. He'll do—"

"Hell's fire!" Jones exclaimed, jumping up. "Stay here," he cried, sloshing on his hat, and lit out like a scorpion had crawled up his pants' leg.

The screen banged shut. Terrazas winced. "Gringos!" he said, wrinkling his nose. Then he thought of his wife and the fine tasty supper she'd be sure to have waiting. He took a glance at his watch. Then, leaning back with a comfortable sigh, he parked his feet on Jones' desk and, in defense against flies, dropped the hat over his face.

All over town they were talking about the fair and the stupidity of dudes who ridiculously imagined a thoroughbred stood any chance against Steeldusts and Travelers at anything under a full half mile. No one liked Grisswell, and not many would have crossed the street for Geetch, but at least he was a product of their environment. A mogul, to be sure, but a man who had come up from nothing. And he was reasonably predictable. Grisswell and most of his help were outsiders. His wealth and his ways made them vaguely uncomfortable. In a manner of speaking they could take pride in Spangler, but Grisswell they resented. So all the smart money was down on Geetch's horse, and the barkeeps were doing a splendiferous business.

The dude's buggy boss had let it be known his employer would cover every nickel put up and they were coming in droves to get in on this gold rush. The man was fair game and everybody figured to get a stake from his disaster.

The fair was due to open tomorrow night and already the town was packed to the gills with folks who'd come early to get in on the fun. Flancher's hotel was crammed solid and every rooming house filled. Jones, on his tour, encountered a mort of strange faces, and not all of these were men.

Something had turned over in Butterfly's mind when the coroner had likened Geetch to a cranky old wolf with one foot in a trap. There still wasn't the least bit of evidence to connect anyone with the theft of Spangler's pony horse. There wasn't a smidgen of proof the dude had been back of it despite Trimbo's claim the tracks had led toward his ranch. But Grisswell had certainly bamboozled Spangler into agreeing to this race, no two ways about that, and had cunningly prodded him into putting up acreage he couldn't afford to lose.

It wasn't the why of this that kept nagging Jones – who could account for a dude's preposterous notions? It was Spangler that bothered him – Spangler's volatile, oft-demonstrated temper. Geetch, if he were desperate enough, would balk at precious little. He was not, Jones thought, the kind to pass up any bets and if he got it in his head there was a chance of Grisswell winning he would take whatever steps seemed most likely to cinch things for himself. *Even to tampering with Grisswell's horse.* And there were plenty of jaspers he could hire to take care of this.

Some such dark purpose may have been the basis of the dude's condescending confidence. The more Jones considered this the more alarmed he grew.

On the face of things there appeared very little likelihood of any thoroughbred running away from one of Geetch's short horses, particularly Eight Below or that flea-bitten mare he called Curtain Raiser. Both were horses Geetch had paid handsome prices for, veteran campaigners in the roughest kind of company, horses he'd been beaten by and then had gone out and bought to make sure it couldn't happen again. By local standards nothing could catch them.

But Grisswell must certainly have known all this. Any feller who'd amassed a fortune from nostrums was not likely to be as big a fool as Grisswell looked. The man had to be convinced he could win.

Jones, tramping the town darkly, completely out of sorts with its holiday mood, believed there had to be an angle hidden somewhere. Grisswell had pushed this thing onto Spangler, setting it up like an arrogant chump, leading with his chin, practically asking to be fleeced. And yet the way in which he'd maneuvered Spangler's acceptance was slicker than slobbers when you hauled off to take a good look at it.

The sheriff, at this point, was reluctantly minded to get on his horse, ride out and have another go at interrogating the man. Not that he imagined anything definitely helpful would come from it. He found Grisswell pretty near as hard to take as Geetch and his bullypuss ramrod. But he couldn't just sit here and wait for that pair to shove a chunk under hell.

Still scowling, he was about to go fetch his horse when he happened to notice Charlie "Rockabye" Mullins backing a spring wagon up against the loading platform of Eph Wilson's Mercantile. Mullins was Geetch Spangler's trainer and had the earned reputation of knowing all there was to be discovered about bangtails.

Though she dressed and frequently employed a brand of language more natural in a man than was generally reckoned proper in a maiden lady, she hadn't stayed with that status on account of being short-changed when the shapes were passed around. In a rough shirt and jeans a feller didn't need glasses to be aware that she was sure female enough.

Nobody denied that she had had a hard life, orphaned at ten, forced to fend for herself amongst a bunch of rough ranch hands.

There was scarcely any basis for comparison between her and, for instance, Cathie Grisswell; but a man couldn't help noticing some of the more manifest differences. Jones recalled the rich fragrance, the crushed violets' smell of the medicine king's daughter, and the intimate cadences of Cathie's hushed voice. He couldn't forget those prickles of excitement.

You'd think a girl, time she got in spittin' distance of thirty, would have figured out some way to get herself up more attractive. Charlie Mullins, he guessed, plain didn't give a damn. Hair skinned back from her ears in that sloppy bun!

Butterfly, peering across the heads of the crowd, wore a concerned and somewhat dubious expression, the look of a kid caught stealing apples.

He'd swapped words with her before, had even taken her to a couple of hoedowns and once had been brash enough to bid in her box lunch, but, in common with most of the unattached males, had found her tongue a little sharp for his taste.

Kind of gritting his teeth he thought of that long ride between him and Geetch's place and began to use his elbows. Approaching the wagon, careful not to stare as she climbed down off her perch, he broke out a smile and said with an assumption of heartiness; "Ain't seen you in a flock of Sundays. What's brought you t' town a day ahead of the fair?"

Pushing a wisp of mousy hair off her cheek, her clay-marble eyes considered his flushed cheeks without noticeable change. "Any special reason you'd be wanting to know?"

"Cripes," he said, nettled, "I was just makin' talk."

"Humph!" she sniffed as though she found it presumptuous, and was turning away when Jones, clenching his fists, kissed caution goodbye, angrily declaring, "It might pay you to remember I'm sheriff of this bailiwick—"

"I'm glad someone finds it a source of satisfaction. Now if you'll turn loose of my arm I've got some chores I'd better tend to."

Butterfly, glaring, licked his lips and said stubbornly, "I want to talk about Geetch—"

"Then you'd better go see him. Geetch and me have parted company."

"Parted . . ." Jones' jaw dropped. "You don't *work* for him anymore?" He peered at her, astounded. "B—but—"

"You're thinking about that race? Geetch won't have any trouble replacing me – he said so himself," she remarked with her lip curled. And, turning her back, she tramped off, leaving Jones standing there.

Chapter Nine

JONES choused up some pretty devastating replies but none of these leapt forth until the object of their venom was safely beyond range. Then he turned the air pink. This let him breathe a little freer but produced practically nothing he could apply to his problems.

Thinking a drink might help he scuffed along to the Purple Cow and was well into his fourth when he chanced, in the back bar mirror, to spot Gattison. Throwing down some change Butterfly caught up his bottle and, picking a somewhat precarious way through the confusion of shifting traffic, dropped into a chair at the little man's table.

The printer, looking put upon, folded both hands across the top of his glass. "Hi, there," Jones said as to an old buddy.

Gattison's reply was an unintelligible grunt, but the sheriff did not let this dampen his grin. He took a pull from his bottle and leaned forward confidentially. "Been aimin' t' look you up, old man. You figured out yet who it was wrecked your plant?"

Eyes darting, the printer mopped at his cheeks, seeming powerfully uncomfortable. A wriggly worm of a man with a scrubby growth across his upper lip and a gray-streaked mane lankly curled about his celluloid collar, the proprietor of Tiedown's now-defunct newspaper looked like something dug out of Skid Row. His bloodshot glance couldn't seem to focus and he squirmed like there were ants in his pants when Jones, setting the bottle off to one side, bent closer to say, "A total loss, was it?"

The man bobbed his head.

"Couldn't save a thing?"

"Well . . ." Gattison said, "I managed to gather up most of the type, but that's about the size of it. No good to me with the press the way it is."

"Couldn't it mebbe be fixed?"

"Those bastards used a sledge! Nothing left of it but junk."

Jones clucked like it had been his own,

84

then said cold as a well chain: "So them broadsheets you got for Hollister Grisswell was printed some while ago. Ain't that right?"

Gattison stared like a frightened mouse.

"Before, in fact, your place was wrecked. Before any race was ever patched up."

It gave a man something to think about. Jones thought about it all the way back to the office. It was pretty unnerving to discover such slyness in a man of Grisswell's wealth and standing, in the father of Cathie, the girl of Jones' dreams. Made a man kind of wonder if there was anything left you *could* tie to.

Dudes, of course, by and large were no more reliable than a woman's watch, but it did seem like, being Cathie's old man, it was pretty underhanded to get that kind of thing printed up and plastered all over before Geetch Spangler even knew there was going to *be* any race. It poked up in Jones' mind a batch of pretty ugly notions.

He found Terrazas, back at the office, about ready to shove off for supper. Allowing it would keep another few minutes, Jones waved the coroner back to his chair. He then went over the talk he'd had with Gattison. "Them handbills was readied, right down to the actual terms of the races, before Spangler that day was bamboozled into it. I tell you, by grab, I don't like the smell of it; the dang thing was up before I got back t' town!"

"It does look a little peculiar," Terrazas nodded, "but it don't break any laws that I ever heard of."

"But how," Jones glared, "could he be so damn confident?"

"Maybe he knows more about Geetch's horse than Geetch does."

"He don't even know which horse he's gonna run!"

"Well . . . I wouldn't bet on that—"

"I was there," Jones growled. "I heard the whole thing. Geetch wanted t' know which horse was to be run an' Grisswell, laughin' told him to pick his best. No horse was named except this thoroughbred the dude calls Jubal Jo. So how *could* he know?"

"Probably knows his own horse."

Jones said, snorting: "You ever heard of a thoroughbred beatin' a cow horse in a quarter-mile go? Try usin' what few brains the Lord has given you!"

Terrazas shrugged. Then blew out his

cheeks. "There's always a first time," he said, getting up.

Jones scrubbed a hand across raspy jowls. "I just can't figure that feller. This whole business stinks, an' it's gonna git worse. Top of everythin' else that dang female has quit – Mullins I'm talkin' about! She—"

"I know." Terrazas nodded. He said, fishy-eyed, "She's hired on with the dude, and I wish that was all, but you better catch hold of something. Sig Raumeller's in town."

Jones couldn't seem to believe his own ears. "You . . . you mean that gun-fightin' son of a bitch that . . . Hell, you got t' be wrong! Even a knothead like Geetch—"

"It was Sig, all right. I watched him get off the stage, saddle guns and batwing chaps."

"Where is he now?"

"Quien sabe?" The coroner sighed. "Last look I had he was headed for the livery."

Jones, spinning round, grayly peered at the screen.

Terrazas said nervously, "I better go eat."

The old hostler at the livery went on with his chores like both of his ears was stuffed full of cotton. Jones' face darkened angrily but he bit back on his temper long enough

87

to be sure the danged old coot had no intention of answering. Then, reaching out, he took hold of him. "I wasn't just talkin' t' find out if I could! When a stranger rents a horse—"

"Didn't rent 'im, he bought 'im."

"He must've asked how—"

"Never ast nothin'. Just paid me an' left." The old man said sullenly, "That's a arm you got hold of—"

"Never mind that," Jones growled, letting go. "Which way was he pointed?"

"With a thousand an' one things t' do around here—? All right, all *right!*" the hostler cried, backing off. "He took the road t' Gourd an' Vine."

Chapter Ten

JONES looked sick. He felt sick, too. All the fears he'd stood off were back, flapping like buzzards round a broken-legged calf.

That goddam Geetch!

Jones fetched out his horse and flung his rig on, swearing bitterly. Wasn't much chance he would get there in time but, as sheriff, he had to try.

All his life Geetch had run roughshod over others, flattening out anything that got in his way. Acting, by grab, like nobody else had any rights at all! Shooting their cows, trampling their crops, burning – even *killing*, when some damn fool was crazy enough to stand up to him. But Jones had never before heard of Spangler fetching in guns from outside to get a job done. Had the crotchety old bastard finally gone off his rocker?

For the first couple of miles Jones applied the steel freely, not taking any time out to wonder what might happen if he did catch up with this two-handed cannonball. When abruptly he eased off it was mostly, he reminded himself, to make sure he wasn't stranded with a give-out bronc.

Some time could be cut off the trip by shortcutting through a prairie-dog town, taking to the brush and kind of nursing the nag along. And Jones thought about this, giving it the best of what attention he could spare during the next several minutes, adding up the pros and cons.

It was getting dark fast and if he stuck to the road there was no guarantee he wouldn't pass the gink up anyhow. Old Sig wasn't the sort to be snuk up on or be took unawares. Killing was his business and he hadn't got where he was with that game taking unnecessary chances.

In a film of cold sweat it came over Price Jones the smartest thing he could do was cut loose of this dido and dig for the tules. A man could get himself croaked mighty quick scissorsbillin' around with the likes of this Raumeller. Where Butterfly sat in the cold ache of that saddle, the prospect of finding himself a dead hero looked anything but inviting.

Nothing he could chouse up to counteract this appeared to have more weight than a gnat's left eyebrow till he banged head-on into the imagined look of Grisswell's Cathie. This wrung a groan from lips that felt considerable drier than a humped-up bale of Confederate cotton. He couldn't haul off and let Geetch's exterminator make an orphan of her. Now, *could* he?

The answer to that did not require much research. He could see plain as paint no man who had red blood in his veins could ride off and leave to fend for herself any girl as sweet as the called-up visions he found fluttering through his mind.

Just the same he rode on, letting the

horse pick its gait for maybe another ten minutes while he stood off the reproaches of an over-anxious conscience before unhappily taking to the brush. A man can shut ears and eyes to a great many things, but an overactive sense of guilt can sure play hob with even a guy like Butterfly Jones, old enough to know better. With a snort of disgust he kicked his mount into a lope, morbidly wondering if Cathie would afterwards still care enough to occasionally, in passing, drop a flower on his grave.

It was close to nine when he raised the ranch's lights. Unlike the rest of the spreads in this godforsaken country, Grisswell's place didn't have to depend on the sort of coal-oil contraptions other folks put up with. He had his place electrified by something that was called a "generator" and had wires run all over, to the astonishment of all who saw them. Breasting the last rise Jones found more lights showing than a man could shake a stick at.

His hopes for this trek skidded down a long spiral, while his belly's empty hollow took on the feel of frogs' legs. That night Grisswell's buggy boss had got him out here before, the only lights showing had been in the owner's quarters. Even the bunkhouse was lit up now. He had a darkly nasty hunch Geetch's gunslinger had got here first.

Got here and gone, he reckoned, deeply sighing. Guessed he might as well ride on in and get it over. Cathie, he opined, was going to take this pretty hard. Whole place, probably, was in a state of shock.

It wasn't until he turned into the yard that the thought came to Jones someone might take a shot at him. Worked up like they'd be over a thing like this – boss cut down right under their noses – this bunch could be jumpy as a boxful of crickets.

He had his mouth half opened when the rove of his glance chanced to pick out at the porch's darkest end a deeper huddle of shadows behind the wink of a spark. Stiffening, staring, he choked off the shout, knees anchoring his horse while he tried to find sense in what he figured to be looking at. Two jaspers sitting there, one of them puffing a quirley or cheroot.

At a time like this.

Smoking, by God!

Seemed pretty near sacrilege the way Jones saw it, trying to rub gooseflesh off the back of his neck. With his eyes like glass chips he took his clamp off the horse and, dropping a hand by the butt of his six-shooter, reined the animal toward them. "Sheriff Jones, here," he called. "You folks havin' trouble?"

"Trouble?" One of that pair on the porch thinly laughed. "Not that we know about. Step down and rest your saddle."

Jones peered harder, about as mixed up now as a feller could get. He felt like a fool. Swearing under his breath he said, "That you, Mister Grisswell?"

"Sounds like you weren't expecting to see me—"

"Who's that up there with you?"

"Come up," Grisswell said. "Like to make you acquainted with the new Gourd and Vine foreman."

Chapter Eleven

JONES, off his horse, stood at the porch's edge, hanging onto his reins and peering at the most notorious notch cutter still making widows in what had been described as "74,000 square miles of pure hell." He was aghast – plumb speechless, at Grisswell's brazen effrontery.

Bad enough, in all conscience, to employ a gink of Sig's stamp in whatever capacity. He found it indescribably worse to think that an owner of Mr. G's educational advantages and commercial accomplishments, *with both eyes open*, could deliberately import and place a cold-blooded killer in a position of authority with so much evident satisfaction.

Jones would sooner have grasped the clawed paw of a hydrophoby skunk than reach out his hand to a pistolero of this stripe – not that Raumeller made any move. The man's bleached stare was no more readable than a snake's, nor did he bother to get up.

Jones, fiddling with his reins while trying to find enough spit to talk with, finally said too loud, "I'd kind of like – if it wouldn't be no great bother – to git me a look at that Jubal Jo horse you're settin' such store by."

"Certainly," Grisswell said, raising up into the light from the windows to pitch his smoke out into the yard. "No bother to me. You want Shores to go with you?"

"Wouldn't want him t' have to hitch up just fer that, I can find my way, I reckon."

And he set off with a wave, glad to get

clear of that pet cobra's stare, but somewhat worried, too, by the bland mocking texture of Grisswell's smile.

He let go of his reins outside the stables, leaving his horse while he went up the runway, finding the place bright as daylight. Horses looked inquisitively around from their stalls, a couple softly whinnying, one pampered bay impatiently pawing a hole the way some running horses will. At the end of the line he found a gray stallion, but the name card tacked beside the Dutch door said *Telachapi Tom*. Nowhere did Butterfly see the black he hunted.

Then he found, somewhat surprised, a door he'd supposed would lead to the clutter of pens out back actually opened into an ell and another double line of stalls, presently dark. Feeling around for a switch he pushed this door open wider. Deep in that darkness he caught the flutter of movement, more heard than glimpsed. Before he could swallow, the place was flooded with light and he found himself gaping at a gimlet-eyed jasper crouched over the gleam of a murderous two-barreled sawed-off shotgun. With twin rasping clicks both hammers went back.

"Hey!" Jones gasped. "Watch out fer that

thing! You wanta *kill* somebody?"

"Wotcher doin' back 'ere?"

"Lookin' fer that horse—"

"Wot I figgered!"

Jones didn't care for the tone of that at all. "Now see here," he cried. "I got a perfect right—" and stopped, jerking round as someone came up beside him. "Cripes, am I glad t' see *you!*" he exclaimed. "Tell that feller, Rockabye . . . ."

The look she gave him would have turned off a tap. "What *are* you doing here?"

She looked pretty grim.

"Well, hell's fire! Dang it, I'm sheriff an'—"

"I expect that's one fact we can't get around." Then she said, "As such you should know this stable's private property."

"Well, sure. Of course it is. Belongs to Mr. Grisswell. He knows I'm here. Told me himself I could . . ."

"All right, Jeeter. You can put up the gun," Charlie Mullins said, and, to Jones: "After what happened to that pony horse of Geetch's you can understand why we've got to take precautions. We got that race coming up. If anything happened to keep Jubal out of it Mr. Grisswell stands to lose ten thousand dollars."

It was as near, Jones guessed, as she could come to an apology. It scarcely made up for the fright he'd been given and did even less toward bolstering his hurt dignity. Still smarting he growled, "I don't have t' be hit over the head to know when I ain't wanted!"

The guy with the double-barreled made a rude noise. With her mousy hair in that untidy bun, the girl lifted her chin to eye Jones' riled face. "Sometimes," she said, "I get to wonderin' about you," and left it lay there between them like a pan of sour dough.

Jones, cheeks darkening, spun to paw for the door. "Hell, don't go away mad," sniggered the clown with the shotgun; and Jones swung back, anger in every outraged line of him.

The Mullins female said with a kind of startled haste, "Come on – I'll give you a knockdown to Jubal," and set off past Jeeter toward the corridor's far end.

Jones, half minded to refuse, scowlingly followed.

By the rear wall she stopped to face the lefthand stall. "There. What do you think of him?"

An arched head came over the door but

Butterfly hardly glanced at the horse. Eyes widening the girl nervously poked at her hair. "Was it Jubal you came here to see or *me?*"

"I'd like t' know why you run out on Geetch . . ."

"That's flattering, I must say. Sometimes, Butterfly—"

"My name's Price, an' I'm not so damn stupid as some people think! Your boss an' Geetch could save a powerful lot of trouble if they'd call off this race."

She peered at him astonished. "You out of your mind?"

"Can't you *see* it? First one thing, then it's half a dozen others, all of 'em calculated t' kick up a feud." He said, softly earnest: "Think back a bit, Charlie. Somebody's *usin'* them two."

For a moment, wide-eyed, she considered him intently, then scorn closed him out. With a sniff she said tartly, "That star's gone to your head."

For a moment it seemed Jones was minded to argue. Then, clamping his jaws, he swung around and tramped off.

Outside, by his horse, he scrubbed a hand across hot cheeks. Snapping up the reins he climbed into the saddle. Without bothering to speak to the pair on the porch he put his horse down the lane, halfway minded to ride on over to Spangler's and see if he couldn't talk some sense into Geetch.

Wrapped in the churn of tumultuous thoughts, at first he didn't notice the shape by the gate, not even when he bent to open the barrier. The first hint he had that he was not alone came with the faint but heady fragrance of crushed violets. Then he saw her standing in the shadows of twin poplars.

He felt a great upsurge of relief. *She* would understand. Her mind wasn't closed against new thoughts like Charlie Mullins', or stunted by pride and intolerance like Spangler's. And she was young enough to listen and weigh a sheriff's words. She had her father's ear. If anyone could help get this stopped it was Cathie.

With so much assurance flowing through his veins, Jones said, "Look – you've got to git your ol' man t' call this race off! An' the quicker the better. This—"

She said: "I couldn't do that." Then, seeing him stiffen, she adopted a more reasonable tone, saying, like Eve giving the nudge to the serpent, "If you think it's the thing to do, I'll talk to him, of course. But you have to realize Daddy has his heart set on this. Ever since we came here people have been telling him what wonderfully fast horses Mr. Spangler has, and how preposterous it is to imagine *any*thing could beat them, least of all a thoroughbred. Why, you'd think to hear them talk that Jubal was some animated freak, fit only to stand at the end of a leadshank.

"Daddy wants people to like him, but he's determined to show them how wrong they are. Jubal was *bred* in speed. For more than five generations all his forebears were celebrated racehorses. His sire is Plaudit, who won the Kentucky Derby. His dam was Cinderella. She has produced more great track performance horses than any mare now alive. And Plaudit's father was one of the greatest speed horses in the history of the turf! Why—"

"Maybe so," Jones broke in, "but the big problem here, far as I'm concerned, ain't got nothin' t' do with who gits beat. It's the hurt feelin's an' hate that race'll work up, an' what it'll do to the country if this outfit an' Spangler decide t' settle things with guns. You better pass on the word; an' if he figures t' stay healthy the very least he kin do is git rid of that gunny—"

"Gunny!" she said with her eyes big and round.

"That new range boss he's hired. That Sig Raumeller jigger . . ."

Even in the uncertain light of these stars Jones glimpsed the startled change in her expression. She seemed to kind of draw back, one hand coming up, while her eyes – great black pearls – swept his face with a dreadful astonishment.

"He'd never do that. You must have rocks in your head."

"But Cathie – the guy's a notch-cuttin' killer!"

"Of course he is. Daddy's no fool!" she cried in a surge of rebellious impatience. "Did you imagine we'd sit here and twiddle our fingers while Geetch Spangler takes this place away from us? The Grisswells have dealt with pirates before!"

Chapter Twelve

JONES went to bed that night with his clothes on. Not expecting to sleep, he lay like a rock, completely out of this world until he woke, half fried with the sun in his face, to find the morning about gone.

Peering blearily, he knuckled stuck-together lids and pushed up, morosely scowling through a series of yawns till his glance chanced to brighten on a near-emptied bottle. Worrying the cork from its neck he held it up to the light and, shuddering, swallowed, belching noisily as he put the thing down.

He finally got up, feeling somewhat more able in a creaky sort of way. Harold Terrazas came through the drag of the screen as he was scraping the last of the soap off his cheeks. "Salud!" the coroner said and grinned sardonically. "I see you got back more or less in one piece."

Jones, dabbing a nick at the side of his jaw, grunted.

"I guess," Terrazas cocked his head, "you must have found Geetch in a down mood for sure, real tore up at being caught in such a caper. Otherwise—"

"I didn't see Geetch. Raumeller," Jones growled, swinging around, "took the road t' Gourd an' Vine."

"That figures. Not much point riding out to see Spangler till he'd earned whatever they settled on. Reckon Geetch'll try to hand him some of that paper?"

Butterfly said fiercely, "This ain't no time for jokes. By grab! When I think of all the ridin' I done tryin' t' save that peckerneck from bein' blown t' dollrags – You know what that dude has done? Made Sig his range boss! Can you beat that fer stupid?"

"He tell you that?"

"Cathie claims 'Daddy' hired him as a kind of insurance!" Jones said, disgusted, "I'd as soon have a goddam rattlesnake around!"

"You tell Grisswell that?"

"I didn't tell him nothin'. Didn't have no chance to with Raumeller settin' right there on the porch . . . I took a look at that horse though. An' that Mullins is pretty near loco as Grisswell. Acts like she figures they got a real chance t' win!"

Terrazas, rubbing his jaw, eyed Jones thoughtfully. "I've a halfway notion to drop a few bucks, you got any spare cash?"

"I sure ain't got none to throw away!"

"Last odds quoted was thirty to one. Man could get well fast with a hundred at that price." He flopped down in the swivel and hung his boots on Jones' desk. "You got to hand it to Geetch, putting that pistolman on Gourd and Vine as range boss. Looks like there's a bite in the old wolf yet."

Jones peered sharply. "You don't really think he done that, do you?"

The coroner shrugged. "It's something to consider. Look back at what's h ppened since you got sworn in. Three hombres stick up the Purple Cow. Ferguson, loaded, gets his light blown out. Both those crimes had a basis in money, and who's short of coin? Plenty of fellows maybe, but Spangler has to be pretty near desperate."

He took down his feet, swiveled up to the desk, got out his pad and picked up a pencil. Jones shook his head. "We don't know that, Harold. And you're forgettin' Gattison."

"We don't even know that Gattison comes into it. Common denominator seems to be money. No money changed hands when that print shop was wrecked. Grudge, maybe. We know Geetch is short. Been paying his hands with I.O.U.'s; saloons have chopped off his credit. Six of his punchers, packing their plunder, took the stage out of here for greener pastures. He's been cock of the walk around Tiedown for years, the Number One Mogul . . . Mister Big himself. What's happened to his wealth? And if he's really in a bind how come he doesn't step around to the bank?"

"He made his pile in cattle," Jones growled. "We've had three years of drought. It's hit all them ranchers, an' Geetch was overstocked. Why, if it wasn't fer the Verdigris River runnin' . . . this whole damn country's about t' blow away! Forced sales have dropped prices – cattle right now is a drag on the market."

Terrazas made some more marks with the pencil. "*His* kind of cattle. Gourd and Vine's got no trouble."

"Whitefaces!" Jones sneered. "Pedigreed stuff raised with kid gloves inside fenced pastures on irrigated grass! Rich man's toys!"

"Takes money," Terrazas nodded. "But the writing's on the wall. They'll all have to come to it—"

"Not Geetch!" Jones said fiercely.

The coroner, smiling, made a couple of squiggles on the pad with his pencil and looked up at Jones blandly. "That's right. Too set in his ways. Too pinched in the cash box. But he's got to do something or go under; in his bust-a-gut way he must have seen this himself. Tries a flyer in horses, finds his luck is still bad. Gets whipped where it hurts. About then, like as not, he's faced with neck meat or nothing.

"He scrapes the bottom of the barrel, groaning up the price to buy the hides that foxed him, and they're good. He wins a few, but the word gets around. They're all talking now about Geetch Spangler's racers. He's had it. Nobody round here will take a run at him."

"There's other places."

Terrazas nodded. "But now he's down to pretty much working with paper. He had a deal on with Rockabye to take Curtain Raiser and that gray, Eight Below, over into Texas where he stood some chance to get well, but that girl's pretty cagey. With the deal still in the dickering stage Grisswell throws that Fair race at him and, quick as he's hooked, hires his trainer away from him.

"Put yourself in Geetch's place. More hay than he can spare and all the best of his range – those Hat Creek sections have been dumped in with the hope of making that dude look like a busted flush. With Mullins he might have done it. But he hasn't got Mullins anymore; the dude's got her."

Jones pawed at his face. Aggravated and scowling he settled his butt against the edge of the desk. "How'd you know he had a deal on with Charlie t' go over into Texas?"

"One thing us Mexicans around here has got is cousins. Happens one of mine is still on Geetch's payroll – Charco Tavares."

Jones' stare was suspicious. "Even so," he finally grumbled, "I can't see where that ties him to this gunhawk."

"Did you know that dude's been buying up Geetch's paper?"

"Where'd you git that?"

"I got to thinking," Terrazas said, "it might give us a line to know how bad Geetch was hurting. So I checked up a little. The Purple Cow, before they shut off his credit, was holding Spangler notes totaling three hundred dollars. He was into the Aces Up for five hundred and ten. Grisswell's buggy boss latched onto both sets. I went over to the Mercantile. Wilson admits Geetch was into him for plenty. He wouldn't say how much but—"

"Did he sell Geetch's paper to Shores?"

"Sold it to someone, and at a pretty good profit from the look in his eye. I found out something else. Shores was in town the day those cowpokes took off. Geetch's debts that I've pinned down will run at close to three thousand. Right now you couldn't—"

"If it's Grisswell—"

"It's not Shores. The fellow hasn't got that kind of dough."

Jones, stewing, fumed. "Why would that dude . . .?"

"He never done it for love."

"But you just as much said *Geetch* was the one put Raumeller over there! I'm so tangled up now—"

"It's kind of tricky," Terrazas nodded, "but who else would profit from having Grisswell killed? It's Spangler that's hurting. Surely you can see that? And the dude's been rubbing salt in his wounds. He's built up a show place right under Geetch's nose; sets him off for the ignorant brush-popper he is. Then he hooks Geetch into this big-stakes race, piles insult on injury by walking off with Geetch's trainer – and don't forget Spangler thinks the dude is responsible for the loss of that pony horse, that Papago Pete some joker run off with. And now this blamed dude is buying up Geetch's notes. Don't it seem like to you a man in Geetch's fix would get to thinking all his troubles could be laid at Grisswell's door?"

Jones looked worried, no two ways about it.

Terrazas said, getting up, "You've got to

see Spangler the way he's been all his life, bellicose and grabby; and the way he sees himself, cow-baron boss of this whole scabby county ... a top dog being hamstrung by a dude."

Chapter Thirteen

PUT that way it did not seem unreasonable to see Raumeller in the cushy saddle of being able to draw pay from two owners simultaneously. So long, anyway, as he could manage to hold off from killing the goose.

Though Terrazas' notions nagged him considerably, Jones wasn't satisfied that such was the case. He couldn't see how Geetch, with that bullypuss temper, could have found enough patience – not to mention savvy – to have planted the man so cleverly on Grisswell. And the dude *had* fetched the leather slapper into this. *Did you imagine*, Cathie had cried, *we'd sit here and twiddle our fingers while Geetch Spangler takes this place away from us!*

Trying to worry some sense from it, Jones

had no idea when Terrazas departed; when he glanced around the coroner was gone. Despite the case the man had built against Geetch it seemed to Jones more likely that both these moguls were considerably at fault, each of them apparently thinking the other was trying to put him out of business. If the dude, as claimed by Terrazas, had been buying Geetch's notes, it was probably no more than as something – like Raumeller – he had done in the hope of keeping Spangler in line.

Jones was not however, encouraged by this to relax in the view that it would all blow away. He was uncomfortably aware how little was needed to nudge this pair into a full-scale feud. He still believed someone else to be back of it, someone maneuvering these moguls to reap personal gain and either pick up the pieces or advantage himself in some other fashion, under cover of the smoke once the guns got to banging.

It was not a pleasant prospect for a man to take to breakfast, and Jones, distractedly reminded of his empty belly, abruptly scooped up his hat with a snort of disgust.

His glance fell across the pad on which Terrazas had doodled. Almost against his will something about the penciled scratchings pulled him closer, and he bent over to stare at the pictured likeness of Spangler's face. All the man's worst qualities had been cunningly captured and frozen into an expression of vindictive hate.

The sheriff, shaken, tore off the sheet and shoved it, grumbling, into his pocket. But the naked savagery of it stayed in his mind to needle him all the way to the restaurant. Was Terrazas right? Was it Geetch's bitter rage that was fomenting all that discord?

If not Geetch, who then? Flancher? Bernagrowt? Eph Wilson, the storekeeper? None of these had the brains or the heft to spur ambition. It was hard to see how any one of them could profit from the turmoil of a range war. A banker might, but Jones could not see Ed Gretchen in the part. The man was too prissy, too chintzy and close, to risk what he had in such an out-and-out gamble. It took a bolder spirit and one twisted by something sharper than cupidity. He was a man more apt to despise than hate.

Gretchen might resent Grisswell, but Spangler's account had nursed him along when no comparable assets had been even in sight. He might refuse Geetch credit in a time tough as this, but Jones couldn't see him engineering Geetch's downfall.

Having padded his ribs the sheriff of Tiedown tramped morosely around to the Purple Cow. The place was being swamped out but he found the owner, O'Halleran, working over his accounts. The Irishman looked up without his usual twinkle. "An' fer what would you be comin' around at this ungodly hour? A nip at the dog that bit ye?"

"Might not be a bad idea," Jones scowled, "but as a matter of fact I'm here on business—"

"No business of mine, I can be sure of that. Go on. Git yer drink an' be off."

A bunching of muscles bulged the sheriff's jaw. "This is *law* business, Eddie—"

"So? Ye've caught them spalpeens that stuck me place up three—"

"Well, no . . . not exactly . . ."

"Didn't figure ye had." The Irishman snorted. "I'll be money ahead to write it off an' fergit it if I got t' depend on the likes of you."

With a hard, scornful glare, he was about to get back to work on his books when Butterfly said on a defensive impulse, "I'll make it up to you—"

"I should live so long?" The Irishman,

sighing, said, "Spare me the fairy tales. Just say what ye've come fer an' git on with it, lad."

"That big winnin' of Ferguson's . . . I understand Spangler was one of the big losers. Didn't I hear he was short of cash?"

The saloon keeper chewed his lip for a moment. "I wasn't playin' that night but I was there; the game had already started when Geetch dropped in. Had a roll in his mit that would choke a giraffe. One twenty folded round a bunch of ones, twos an' fives." O'Halleran sniffed. "The boys weren't too happy an' got some agg'avated when Mahls took the wad an' set ten blues in front av him. You could tell Geetch was hungry. There was a slug of paper in that game when they finished."

"How much'd he stick you for?"

A kind of sour smile walked across the man's mouth. "Didn't take me fer any that night – nor Mahls. Jack had already told him he was through playin' bank before Shores got onto us. All I had was six months of his bar chits."

"Five hundred an' ten bucks worth? He swill that much likker in—?"

"Him an' his hands." O'Halleran nodded. "They been drinkin' like fish. How'd . . .

Terrazas told you, eh?"

"How much of Geetch's paper did that leaser go off with?"

"Fifteen hundred . . . coupla thousan' mebbe."

Jones stared at his thoughts. "Well, thanks," he said. "I'll see if I can't git a lead on them stickups."

"Don't strain yerself, boy," O'Halleran said, and Jones flushed.

Back in the sun he mulled it over some more. Thing had more angles than a dog had fleas. Had the stickup at O'Halleran's been part of the whole, or just an isolated incident like the sledgehammer smashing of Gattison's press? Could a man even be sure that that had no connection with the animosity stirred up between Geetch and Grisswell?

Terrazas had dismissed it as the work of a crank. But Gattison had held Geetch up to censure before. When the Twiddler family had been run off their place the paper had carried a bristling editorial, asking how long would people stand for Spangler's bullying. Been no love lost between them two. And busting up that press had been just the kind of stunt a man would look for Geetch to pull.

With such an influx of strangers in town for the Fair, as sheriff, Price Jones felt it incumbent to keep himself in circulation. The county's annual whingding was due officially to open this evening at six with a display of baked tasties, patchwork quilts, hooked rugs, rag rugs, fudges and taffies, leather goods and whatnot. Tomorrow's schedule included bronc riding, bull riding, wild-cow milking and roping, plus three matched races – in addition to the much publicized quarter-mile dash between Geetch and the dude.

Terrazas was also policing the crowds. Jones saw him several times during the course of the afternoon, though never near enough to speak with. There were a lot of hard faces moving through the jostling throngs. Twice he had to break up fights. At five-thirty, feeling like something dragged through a knothole, he went round again to the Lone Star Grub, and climbing onto a stool at the oilcloth-covered counter, proceeded through habit to feed his face.

At six, he was irritably back on the street and, at six-fifteen, gravitating toward the livery where, to ease aching feet, he picked up his horse. He could not shut off the worrisome thoughts that hung in his mind like a clutch of bats. He could feel the tension the way a patched bone feels the approach of a storm. Its brittle grip was in the pinched shine of faces, the too boisterous laughter. Had Spangler, desperate, killed that leaser for the poker winnings that had bulged the man's pockets? Did anyone besides Terrazas suspect him?

Where else could he have got hold of the cash he had bet on the outcome of tomorrow's race? From the bank? On a mortgage perhaps? Was he one of the three who'd stuck up the Purple Cow? Was the theft of that pony horse really a felony or just something cooked up to give him an excuse to tie into Grisswell?

Questions. Questions. They were thicker than coyotes around a lost lamb! How else could Geetch have gotten the money, though? During the afternoon, checking both saloons, Jones had made it his business to look into that betting. Spangler, covering odds against his horse Eight Below, had put up with the barkeeps – in hard coin of the realm – more than twenty-two hundred dollars!

Most of the jostling throngs had by this time begun to drift in the direction of the stockyards where, in the big auction barn built of corrugated tin, the competition in exhibits had been set up for display so that folks would be able to watch the judging. Jones reckoned he had better perambulate over there.

He would have liked to been able to sit down with Geetch and thrash out some of these things he found so uncomfortable to contemplate. But a man could just as well talk to a rock as expect to get any change out of Spangler. It had become one of the established facts of life around here that in his cattle-baron role Geetch did the asking. He was above giving answers.

Jones shook his head. When Geetch came up against something a glare couldn't whip, his likeliest reaction was to reach for a gun.

Riding his horse about the fringes of the crowd for a while, listening to the snatches of talk and keeping both eyes peeled to spot and stop trouble before it could get out of hand, an hour or so later Jones found himself staring at Geetch.

The rancher had two of his hands in tow, both hard specimens, standing back and watching the yokels with that sour tolerance which had become so much a part of him. It was the first time the sheriff had caught a look at the man since that day at Gourd &

Vine when, at Trimbo's insistence, he'd gone out there over the matter of Geetch's missing pony horse and wound up accepting Cathie's invite to lunch.

It wasn't at all likely the old man had forgotten. Or forgiven it, either. In Spangler's book Jones' refusal to ride off with him had gone down either as rebellion or the whim of a stupid fool. A black mark, for there were no shades of gray in the cattle king's judgment of other folks' motives. You either walked where Geetch said or prepared for the consequences.

Considering this, Butterfly regarded the thought of confronting him with something less than outright enthusiasm. It just didn't seem like the right time to do it. Geetch's normally ruddy face seemed more than usually belligerent, and there was a bitterness in him – a kind of barren coarseness seeping through the hard twisted cast of his features that was visible even from here.

Jones, dryly swallowing, excused himself on the grounds that really there was nothing he could say. There was no evidence against the man, nothing that would stand up in a court of law. If Terrazas' contentions had any basis at all, or Cathie's voiced suspicion, the most obvious start for uncovering Geetch's guilt might well lie in the whereabouts of that allegedly missing pony horse.

Jones wondered why he hadn't happened onto this notion before.

But where would a man start looking?

If the horse hadn't been stolen it seemed a pretty good bet the animal probably had been penned up someplace inside the confines of Spangler's ranch. And, in that case, it seemed to Jones, the coroner's cousin, Charco Tavares, would be the man to get in touch with. And right now, by grab, while Geetch was here in town, looked the best time to take a stab at it.

Unaware that the rancher had observed his prolonged scrutiny, Jones, still thinking about Tavares and the missing Papago Pete, reined his mount away from the barn and jogged off uptown on a hunt for Terrazas.

He went first to the two saloons and, not finding him there, cut back toward the combination office and jail. Dusk was beginning to darken the view and several shopkeepers had got their lamps lit in the hope of enticing into their tills some of the out-of-town dollars still restively tramping the warped plank walks.

The office was filled with thickening

shadows. Even so Butterfly put his head around the screen before he would believe the coroner wasn't there. It was much too late for him to have gone home for supper. He wasn't on the street and, after watching awhile, it seemed equally unlikely the man would be found in one of the stores.

Tempted to give it up, the sheriff considered the street once more. He didn't want to jeopardize the project by leaving a note which anyone who happened into the office might read. So far as was known the man was happily married, but Jones, ever a lukewarm believer in the theory of wedded bliss, on a sudden hunch climbed back in the saddle and kneed his horse toward the south end of town.

A well-beaten path led off through the brush that concealed Tiedown's shame. There, behind closed shutters in an unpainted cluster of whoppyjawed shacks, the madams conducted their clandestine business. But though he knocked at every door no one admitted having seen Terrazas and, disgruntled, Jones reckoned any hands left at the ranch would be in bed time he got there.

Angling back toward the stockyards in this uncertain light he was rounding the rear of Bernagrowt's saddle shop when something whipped past his ear with the whine of a hornet. In that split second of frozen astonishment – even before he could reach up to cuff at it – a gun's flat crack viciously broke from the alley.

Jones, yelling, raked the horse with his spurs and, flattening himself as much as he could, drove his mount full tilt into the first hole available. This was the slot between the Dutchman's west wall and the adjacent Lone Star Grub.

Careering into the street, pistol naked and lifted, the first thing Jones saw in the light from the storefronts was the barrel-chested shape and startled face of Spangler's range boss.

Chapter Fourteen

TRIMBO did not have the street to himself. There were other dark shapes stiffly caught in Jones' stare, fixed as the figures in a wax museum – even a fringe-topped surrey behind matched bays, eyes rolling with fright, in the brittle hush; but it was

121

Spangler's man who drew and held the sheriff's attention.

The matched pair moved. The spell was broken as additional people, some running, most of them avidly gaping, converged on the scene with a clatter of questions inspired by thrill-hungry, morbid curiosity.

Neither Trimbo nor Jones gave them any kind of notice.

Jones made no move to get out of the saddle. In headlong anger he furiously cried: "You throw that shot at me?"

Trimbo shook his head like a man confused. His tongue licked out and crossed parched lips. He swallowed a couple of times and said in the voice of a man shook from sleep, "I'm right where I was when the sound of it stopped me—"

"All who believe that kin stand on their heads!"

"Man it's the *truth*. Take a look at my gun—"

"You snake-eyed son of a bitch," Jones snarled, "the truth ain't in you!"

Trimbo took it in silence. They could all see Jones was aching to shoot. Spangler's man hoarsely said, "If you'd look at my gun . . ."

Some measure of caution must have

seeped through Jones' rage. Still reared in the stirrups like a scorpion with its tail up, he said more reasonably: "All right. Pass it over."

Trimbo drew a full breath. Approaching in the manner of a wet-footed cat, the Quarter Circle S ramrod gingerly drew the pistol from its anchorage in his belt and, grasping the weapon by its barrel with his left hand, stopped beside the shoulder of Jones' mount to hand it up.

Butterfly lifted the muzzle and grimly sniffed. It was plain the Colt had not recently been fired, but this didn't mean the range boss did not have another smaller weapon concealed about him somewhere.

With his own .44 tucked under his arm Jones broke open Trimbo's pistol, shook out the loads and dropped them in his pocket. Knowing he could not search the man here without piling up risks he didn't have to take, he tossed the empty weapon back. With his own gun resettled in his fist he said: "Expect you better come down to my office."

The man scowled. "What for?"

"We'll look into that more careful when we git there. Start walkin'."

Something relieved, almost slyly amused,

briefly flickered in Trimbo's considering stare. Then he shrugged and struck off.

Sitting back in his saddle Jones walked the horse after him, narrowly watching for tricks. But as he wheeled past the surrey a glance up the reins surprisedly widened on the face and approving smile of Cathie Grisswell. Warmed by this he touched his hat, and, feeling a little foolish about the pistol, put it away.

He supposed she and her parent had come in to see the exhibits, though Grisswell himself was not presently visible. Jones was flattered to think such important people were not above openly registering their interest. He knew well enough what a poor figure he cut in the eyes of these penny-pinching counter-jumping merchants – you wouldn't see none of them rushing forward to help him!

He hoped Terrazas would be at the office, but he wasn't. The place was still dark when Butterfly told Trimbo to stop by the steps. Swinging down in the shadows he ducked under the rail, having anchored the horse, and was about to order Spangler's range boss inside when the he-coon himself stepped out of the night with a blustery growl, "What the hell's goin' on here?"

It caught Jones off balance, and while he was trying to find wind enough to talk with Trimbo said, "It looks like a shakedown—"

"Now wait a minute," Jones snarled. "Some joker took a shot at me out back of Bernagrowt's, an' when I come larrupin' into the street this character was roundin' the front of that shop—"

"Why don't you tell him the truth?" Trimbo jeered. "I was just walkin' past, and I wasn't the only one. There was anyways five or six other guys out there."

Spangler was in a real sod-pawing mood. His back was arched like a mule in a hailstorm and the veins stood out thick as ropes on his neck. But Jones had some spleen of his own to get rid of. "If you was so dadblamed innocent," he cried, "what'd you stop fer when I come outa that alley? Hah? Answer me that! Them others musta thought you'd run into a wall."

"The look of you on that horse, jaws flappin', eyes flamin', was enough to cramp anyone," Trimbo came back. "I thought, by Gawd, you'd gone clean off your rocker."

"Never mind my rock – you just git up them steps," Jones snarled, skinning his teeth, "or I'm liable t' forgit what I'm packin' this badge fer!"

While his trouble-shooter hesitated, looking half-way minded to test the sheriff's mettle, Spangler, rearing up, appeared about to flip his lid. "You can't jail a man for starin'!" he shouted. "What the goddam hell're you tryin' to *do* t' me!"

"You better take a look at what you're doin' to yourself," Jones advised, sounding testy. "It won't hurt this feller to spend a night in the jug—"

But the Quarter Circle S owner, waving his arms and half-strangled, yelled: "I ain't thinkin' about *him!* We got a race t' run tomorrer an' a horse t' keep our eyes on, an' after what happened t' Papago Pete—"

"Alls I want," Jones cut in, but Spangler, bellowing like a sore-backed bull, drowned him out. "I don't care about that! *You can't have him now!* Until we're done with that race I want him down at the stockyards—"

"Too bad about you. There's folks is plumb fed up with your wants," Jones grated, too riled to curb the churn of his bile. "All their lives they been jumpin' through the hoops for Quarter Circle S, bowin' an' scrapin' like a bunch of goddam monkeys! You ain't God A'mighty, Spangler! Now git the hell away from here before I run you in!"

It looked for a bit as though the rancher would go for his gun. No one before had ever spoke to him so free, and his old man's face took on the kind of splotchy pallor of a gent not two breaths away from having a stroke.

His eyes bulged like squeezed grapes. His mouth worked, and the skin hanging in wrinkles below the jut of his trembling chin lifted and dropped like the wattles of a gobbler, but nothing came out that a man could make any sense of.

Jones, spinning around, gave Trimbo such a shove toward the steps, the man, caught in the lock of his spurs, went down with a thump that shook the whole porch.

You talk about mad!

Trimbo's lips peeled back from his fangs like a snake's. The hiss of his breath was like a snake's too, but the rage-blurred hand making a pass for his belt suddenly stopped in mid-motion when he found himself gaping into the snout of Jones' gun. "Go ahead," Jones drawled – "don't wait on me!"

Chapter Fifteen

A SIZABLE crowd half ringed them in. Jones, irritably eyeing the nearer faces, said, "All right, sports, fun's over. Break it up," and watched them draw reluctantly off. A bunch of goddam sheep, he thought, listening to the receding mutter and mumble. Small wonder Spangler took them for fools. Dropping the hip-held .44 into its scuffed holster he took a hard look at Trimbo and shook his head. "You might as well git goin' too."

Shouldering past he went up the steps, yanked open the screen and passed into the gloom of the unlighted office. Still in the clutch of his sour disenchantment he was reaching for the lamp when the tail of his glance picked out the black hulk of a shape against the window.

"For Pete's sake what are *you* doin'?" he growled.

Terrazas, putting the shotgun aside, said on a sigh of letgo breath, "If he'd touched that pistol I was figuring to blast him loose of his britches."

"Trimbo?" Jones, staring, snorted. "Guess you're no brighter than the rest of us yokels. No more harm to that guy than you'd find in a sparrow."

The coroner said anxiously. "You been working too hard?"

Jones found the lamp, scratched a match and got it lit. "I been too close to the woods t' see the kind of timber that's growed up around us."

"What's that supposed to mean?"

"Where the devil have you been? Did you know I looked all over for you?"

"Was afraid you might. I didn't dare leave a note." Terrazas sat tiredly down on the cot. "Let me catch my breath. What's all this about Trimbo?"

"We been diddled," Jones growled. "The guy's a fourteen-carat fake. Looks tough, sounds tough, with no more guts than a sackful of straw. They've took in the whole range with that bleach-eyed bum."

"He didn't look like no bum when he was going for that pistol."

"That's what's made him so important to Geetch. I been as scared of that whippoorwill as any damn kid in three-cornered pants. But never again!" Jones tossed a handful of cartridges onto the desk. "That gun was dehorned an' both of us knowed it."

Terrazas seemed doubtful, and gruffly said, "He's done some pretty rough things for a guy without guts."

"That kinda stuff comes easy when you're holdin' the whip hand."

"Then you think it's all Geetch?"

"I don't know what I think." Jones glared at his fists as though minded to break something. "Where was you when I was combin' this town?"

"Quarter Circle S – probably on the way back. I went out to see Charco." The coroner said, leaning forward: "We found that horse."

"Spangler's lead pony?"

The Mexican nodded. "Dead as hell in the bottom of a gulch. Birds had been at him but it was Pete, all right . . . You don't look too excited," he said.

"Stood to reason he'd been on Spangler's range someplace. But that don't mean Spangler put 'im there."

"It don't?" Terrazas studied Jones with his head to one side. "What does it take to convince you, man?"

"More'n I've had my nose rubbed in so far."

They stared at each other while the silence piled up and the wind outside pulled groans from the rafters. "Look at it," Jones said. "All of a kind. Everything we turn up seems t' point square at Geetch. Don't that appear kind of strange to you?"

"No," Terrazas said. "Not to me it don't. That old mossyhorn has been boss in these parts since about the year One. Only guy round that don't eat out of his hand is that dude. He don't have to and it's burned Spangler up. He can't abide Grisswell's guts."

"So you figure he took an' killed his own horse to put Grisswell on a limb he could saw out from under him?" Jones said morosely. "Afraid I can't buy it."

"What you see shaping here doesn't rest on that. Grisswell's maneuvered him into a race, set the conditions himself . . . stakes Geetch would hate to lose. Stakes he can't afford. Then this loco dude hires his trainer away. On top of everything else the man's hard up for cash. Half his crew walks off. Then Grisswell sends Shores around buying up his notes—"

"You make almost as good a case against the dude, and I'd as soon suspect him as this nizzy old fool that's put his back to the wall to buy a bunch of crazy bangtails he's got no goddam use fer." Jones blew out his cheeks in an irritable sigh. "It just goes t' prove what I been sayin' all along.

131

Somebody wants them two t' lock horns an' they're just crossgrained enough t' pitch in an' help."

"All right," Terrazas said. "Who you puttin your chips on? Eph Wilson the storekeeper? How'll it help him? The proprietor of Tiedown's plush hotel? Bernagrowt the saddlemaker?"

"There's other people lives around here that could profit."

"I can't think of no one but Gretchen the banker and a range war wouldn't do *him* too much good."

"Oh, I don't know," Jones grumbled. "It would give him an excuse to pick up some pretty fair spreads for the price of foreclosure."

"You think it's him?" Terrazas looked his astonishment.

"Hell, no. But I could easier think it was him than Geetch. Mebbe I'm stubborn," Jones said grumpily, "but I just can't see a guy out to make trouble leavin' himself as wide open as Geetch is."

"Maybe you ought to look again at his past. You see anything hidden about the way he got his land?"

"He sure never wishy-washied around like this!"

"Probably cramped his style when all them boys quit—"

"I'll tell you one feller could profit. An' he could be sore at both of 'em – Gattison."

They sat a while considering it. "He's a terrier," the coroner, frowning, admitted. "He gets hold of a thing he's hard to shake loose. It could be the reason he got put out of business. . . ."

"But the guy," Jones went on, "puts the goose bumps on me is that damn Sig Raumeller. Deal like this is just made for his kind."

"Which brings us right back to Geetch," Terrazas nodded. "Where there's so much smoke there's got to be some fire, and he's the one guy that's really hurting. He's been hit with more luck, and all of it bad, than the rest of them laid end to end put together. A few fresh stiffs strewed around through the brush wouldn't no more bother him than worms in his biscuits. A shooting war—"

"F' pete's sake, Terrazas, you got Geetch on the brain!"

"Close your eyes if you want to, but facts is facts and you can't get around them," the coroner said doggedly. "There's plenty of evidence—"

"The man is bein' framed."

"You don't believe he's hard up?"

"I never said that."

"Then where'd he get the twenty-two hundred he's put up at the bars to cover that race!"

Chapter Sixteen

JONES tossed and turned half the night until finally, desperate, he got up and hit the bottle. Even that was no better than a temporary crutch. It let him get to sleep but the morning found his problems just as big and black as ever. Considerably blacker, even more pressing, because today was the date of that confounded race. And one thing he'd certainly got to face up to. If Geetch wasn't the skunk hid under this wood-pile, they were faced with the necessity of providing an alternative.

He kind of wished now he had let Gretchen sack him.

His legs weren't too steady and his head howled like the inside of a stamp mill as he scooped up his hat and clapped his shell belt around him. All the way to the Lone Star Grub the pound in his head kept banging away at that one stinking word. *Who?*

Who had set this pot boiling? Who, besides Geetch, could look to better his condition by stirring these antagonisms? Who had known enough about either of their wants and needs and personal involvements to prod these two moguls into each thinking the other was out to do him in?

He supposed uneasily it *could* be Gattison, but he didn't much like it. The printer was a little terrier of a man and, in his capacity as editor of Tiedown's now-defunct newspaper, had sometimes waxed pretty pompous. But, to Jones' way of thinking, the feller was a windbag and more like to take his resentments out in talk than involve himself in this kind of dido. Gattison seemed too peppery to be possessed of either the patience or cunning.

Not that Jones didn't plan to have some words with him once the more urgent of his chores were out of the way. He planned to see Charco, too, but figured first of all he'd better get in touch with Grisswell. The most explosive element in this whole situation – as Butterfly saw it in his own mind – was that hired gunny, Raumeller, and if there

135

was any way of parting him from Grisswell's company the sheriff reckoned he ought to do it before somebody got killed.

Jones wasn't particularly hungry when he plopped himself down on one of the Lone Star's stools, but he got into a conversation with the local Butterfield agent and became so engrossed in his speculations that before he got up he'd put away two eggs, a thick slab of steak, four pieces of toast, three cups of java and a pretty fair chunk of gooseberry pie. More miraculous still, he got shed of his headache.

Gattison, it seemed, had been making enquiries concerning stage connections which had necessitated checking with a number of other lines. While nothing appeared to be firm yet, and neither money nor ticket had crossed the counter, the points being aimed at – the agent told Butterfly – were Butte, Montana, and Deadwood in the Dakotas. Moreover the printer, Jones was told, had not even been near the Butterfield office. The go-between had been a nine-year-old, one of the Potter brood of broken-down whites camped out in Rag Holler ever since Trimbo had run them off a quarter section of Geetch's land.

This sort of thing looked pretty hush-

hush to Jones and fetched several growls as he headed for the livery to pick up his horse. Thinking back he remembered the Potters had been moved three years ago . . . about the same time Spangler's crew had burnt the Olafsons out.

But if Gattison intended to shake the dust of this town why not just *do* it? Who was he trying to hide it from? Geetch?

"Trimbo . . ." Jones said, thoughtfully frowning. Strangely enough the man hadn't previously come into his consideration of possible suspects. Nor could Butterfly think why he'd so easily dismissed him after that business last night out back of Bernagrowt's.

It had been a mighty close thing he was grimly reminded, gingerly touching the nicked ear's abraded skin. Jones had let the man go in bitter disgust after Spangler got into it . . . because of the bluff Geetch's range boss had run with an empty gun?

There had been no proof Trimbo had taken that shot at him; no evidence on the other hand to prove that he hadn't, *and who was closer to Geetch than Trimbo?* Who would know better how to stir up Geetch's fury, how to play on his weaknesses, feed his angers? And it wasn't as though that unfired iron the sheriff had unloaded gave the feller a clean bill of health. He could easily have had another cached about him. Jones remembered now he'd been intending to look – and a golrammed pity he hadn't!

The feller had been near enough – and at the right time, too, to have thrown those slugs that had killed the dude's mare. There was a number of things, Jones was suddenly discovering, which – with Trimbo as prime mover – appeared to drop into place.

All the time he was saddling up the sheriff poked and prodded Trimbo for size. He looked a pretty apt fit; the biggest thing really lacking, Jones concluded, was motive, and a little judicious digging might uncover that, too.

But Gattison, also, was beginning to make rather far-apart tracks. If these enquiries stemmed from the smashing of his press why was he being so secretive? And why hadn't he up and gone before this? The man had known straight off the press was irreparable. What dark facts could the man have nosed out?

If the press had been destroyed to put the paper out of business . . . Jones, shaking his head, went into the saddle. A hint drastic as that would have been sufficient to shut most mouths, and it appeared to have shut Gattison's. Jones, when he'd talked with him had certainly not got anything worth writing home about.

But if what he'd nosed out had been sufficiently damaging mightn't the printer have tried a bit of blackmail? This, in conjunction with the man's known character, seemed to Jones to be a reasonable assumption. Seemed to tie in, too, with those guarded enquiries into stage connections. So what was he waiting for?

The loot, of course!

It came down on Jones like a ton of brick. The man was waiting for the payoff.

The cocky little bastard!

With cold sweat breaking through the pores of his skin, Jones, suddenly snarling, kicked a grunt from his gelding. Half a minute later he jumped off at the middle of town and, knocking men off his elbows, bucked his way into the hotel-lobby, making straight for the desk in a spur-chinging stride.

"You seen Gattison this mornin'?"

Flancher looked startled, worriedly shook his head.

"What room's he in?"

"Second floor back – Number Ten . . ."

Jones took the stairs like a herd of buffalo, made the bend for the ell and banged on the panels of the door chalked 10. He got nothing but sore knuckles. Dang fool was probably gone to the cattle judging, but just to make sure he wasn't still abed sleeping, the sheriff tried the door and, finding it unlocked, shoved it open.

He saw the shape on the bed and swore.

Gattison wouldn't trouble no one anymore.

Chapter Seventeen

BUT, having locked the door and pocketed the key, Jones stood awhile, frowning, gone back in his thinking again to Trimbo and the dark shape of Spangler stiffly standing behind him. His breakfast was not riding too smooth and there was a brassy taste in his throat like bile. Be powerful easy to go off half-cocked.

And tramping down the stairs, with all those staring faces peering up at him, he couldn't help wondering at the strange compulsion he felt, even now, to heave away any hint of Geetch's guilt. Somebody sure as sin had took hold of that printer, angrily, viciously, to shut his mouth.

"Was he there?" Flancher asked.

"He was there," Jones said, and the whole damned lobby appeared to hang on his words. He beckoned Flancher aside. "Anyone asked fer 'im?"

The hotel man shook his head. "Something wrong?"

"You think there might be?"

"Well," Flancher grumbled, "you look kinda odd."

"Don't lit it worry you, and stay away from that second floor. Don't let nobody up there. An' keep your lip buttoned. I'm sendin' Terrazas over soon as I can find him."

He went out on the porch, eyes quartering the street. He didn't know what he expected to find, but whatever it was he couldn't set his teeth in it. Things looked about the same . . . traffic a little heavier, maybe.

He moved down the steps and got on his horse, and presently turning him into the flow, sandwiched him through and cut left toward the jail. Quite a few of the jabberers he saw on the walks appeared to be drifting in the direction of the stockyards, though the races weren't scheduled to start before one.

A glance at his shadow showed it wasn't yet ten.

Dismounting beside the jail he went into his office, his narrowed stare finding his deputy doodling at the desk. "Sort of figured you'd be out policing the street."

Terrazas, looking up, blew the sweat off his nose. "Didn't seem much use in both of us roasting. Saw you go past as I was—"

"Gattison," Jones said, "ain't no longer with us."

"You mean he packed up and—"

"Somebody scrambled his brains with the barrel of a six-shooter."

Astonishment twisted half the lines of Terrazas' face and then a blankness clamped down and his unreadable eyes considered Jones steadily while the clock on the wall continued solemnly to mark the passage of time. He said abruptly, "Gattison!" like it didn't make sense.

Though he was not quite able to put his fist on the reason, it got into Jones' mind there was something dimly off-key about this performance. "The guy tried to put somebody over a barrel. But he fiddled too long an' the heat caught up with him."

Terrazas' glance widened. "You suggesting he was trying to collect *hush* money?"

"Looks that way." Jones told the coroner what he'd found out from Butterfield's man. "He was fixin' t' skip soon's he feathered his nest. You better git over there."

He tossed Terrazas the key.

The man opened his mouth, apparently thought better of it, shrugged and departed.

Now what was he fixing to say? Jones wondered, pondering the coroner's final, dubious look. Likely something about Geetch.

Darkly scowling Jones hauled the sketch of Spangler from his pocket and, smoothing it out, studied, deeply uneasy, the penciled likeness. He found it pretty persuasive. The kind of look you'd expect to find on the face of a man who would beat another man's head in.

Still frowning, the sheriff climbed into the saddle. He didn't know what to do, really; whether to hunt up Grisswell or go see Geetch.

He peered at his watch. The hands said ten-thirty. Jones had never found Spangler an easy man to talk to and, remembering the way they had parted here last night, he entertained no illusions concerning his probable reception.

For the benefit of fairs the county had scraped a half-mile oval just north of the stockyards, erecting one rail of peeled poles – presently whitewashed – around this bullring's outside perimeter. On the nearer side, between it and the stockyard pens and chutes, a saddling paddock in the form of a wheel made of warped mesquite lengths had been thrown up beside ten tiers of jerry-built bleachers. Beyond the track's far side, amid considerable activity, were the flimsy, weatherbeaten structures locally known as Shed Row. It was for these, still scowling, that Jones pointed his horse.

Among mounds of baled hay, battered tubs of water, acridly pungent heaps of mixed manure and bedding, those involved went on with the chores attendant to getting a race under way. Flies were everywhere, buzzing and circling over refuse and feed, and the area was additionally cluttered by the curious, bookmakers and bettors and those who – the largest number – had gratuitously come to offer their counsel.

Off to one side Charlie Mullins was walking a powerful-looking black stallion with a white star and snip. Several other horse walkers slouched along in procession. Between these and her, Jones observed the Grisswell stable hand, Jeeter, eyes fiercely alert above the dark tubes of his twin-barreled Greener.

From the vantage of his saddle, Jones peered around, hoping to catch sight of Cathie's father, and presently did so. But the Gourd & Vine owner, when Jones' glance ran him down, was over by the sheds, deep in talk with Sig Raumeller. The sheriff watched them awhile, thinking Grisswell would presently be done and one or the other of them move to someplace which might allow a more casual approach. After fidgeting for several minutes under the stare of the gun fighter Jones wheeled his mount and went looking for Geetch.

He found the Quarter Circle S owner holding forth in a group of well-wishers who had money on his horse. The talk derisively revolved about Grisswell and the consensus of opinion seemed to have the dude's thoroughbred whipped to a standstill before he so much as set foot on the track.

Jones was reluctant to intrude on this pleasure but he had either to speak with someone pretty quick or wash his hands of the whole upsetting business, at least so far as trying to avert hostilities went.

Lips drawn into a distasteful grimace he kneed his horse over, hearing the talk fall away as people discovered his presence.

Spangler did not help him. With his pale squinted stare bleakly fixed on the sheriff the rancher stood waiting, belligerently silent, putting the whole burden of any exchange on Price Jones.

But Jones, now that he had the cattle king's attention, could not seem to find any reasonable approach. He had vaguely thought he might point out in a general sort of way the dangers the race could produce. Face to face with Geetch the whole idea looked a bit preposterous. Nor could he ask the rancher to withdraw from the race.

He cleared his throat self-consciously. "You fellers hear about Gattison gettin' knocked off?"

There was no sign of shock. Though Jones had put it to the group he'd kept his glance pinned to Geetch and got no change at all. A couple of the others looked mildly surprised but no one offered any vocal contributions.

"That's straight," Jones affirmed, cheeks beginning to burn. "I ain't pullin' your legs. He was found in his room at the Drover's

Rest, dead in his bed with his head bashed in."

Spangler made no bones of his contemptuous indifference. "Small loss," he declared. "Man's been askin' for that ever since he come here." Then his stare beating harder against Jones' face, he said with an unmistakable sneer, "Did you reckon *I* had anything to do with it?"

That bleached-agate stare was no easy thing to meet and Jones visibly squirmed. But he did not back off. Fully seeing the trench he might be digging for himself, he told the cattle king, "Your past performances sure ain't been above reproach."

Spangler's neck and chest swelled while the rest stared askance and the rancher's bloating features took on the color of fury. Then a scornful bark of a laugh leaped out of him. "F' Christ's sake, Jones! When you goin' t' grow up?"

That was pretty hard to take, hard in any circumstance but doubly so with these yaps looking on, storing it up to pass around later. But Jones hung on, not letting Geetch throw him. "We're talkin' about you an' that dead guy, mister. You can talk t' me or you can talk to a warrant."

Chapter Eighteen

TO himself Jones sounded astonishingly firm, a hard-held restraint wearing noticeably thin in the harshening tones of that delivered ultimatum.

Sheerest kind of bluff. Inside, aghast, he was a quagmire of squirming, quivering contradictions, unsure even if he had any basis for threatening arrest.

And this blustery old man, no matter anything else, was still the county's Number One citizen, paying the most taxes, entitled by such to the veneration, allegiance and unfaltering support of each and every county official. They were all part and parcel of the Spangler power and influence, prerogatives of the mighty.

Preposterous twaddle? Well, perhaps. Certainly no such feudal notions could be found in the ordinances and lawbooks, but their shadows hedged in every lawman's horizon, circumscribing his authority, stronger than wire. And it looked like Geetch was desperate.

But Jones had *his* back against a wall, too. For if Spangler had any hand in what had happened to that printer he was almost certainly concerned with the rest – the Purple

Cow stickup, the wrecking of Gattison's press, Ferguson's death and, by the same token, that pair of slugs which had been thrown at Grisswell. It was all of a piece in Price Jones' head and he was faced with the job of getting at the truth of it. *And if Geetch wasn't guilty he had the right to be cleared.*

The old man's look, still livid, seemed somehow more cagey, and now he said in a more disciplined way, "I'm a reasonable man. Ask your questions; *I've* got nothing to hide."

"Where was you last night?"

"Part of the time I was out to the ranch. Bulk of the night right here on Shed Row, rolled in my soogans hard ag'in that door." The lifted sweep of rope-scarred hand indicated the closed lower half of one of the stalls, over which a gray tail jerked occasionally at flies.

"You never went to the hotel?"

Spangler said, snorting, "With the kind of stakes I got sunk in this race you think I'd leave Eight Below here alone!"

"You could have left Trimbo with him."

"Trimbo was off uptown – you know that."

"I seem to recall seein' *you* uptown, too.

At around ten o'clock in front of the jail. When the three of us was havin' that powwow, who was watchin' your horse?"

"I'd just rode the horse in—"

"You weren't mounted when I talked with you."

"The horse right then was with two of my boys. They was right in plain sight if you'd troubled to look."

Sweat lay damply across the ridges of Geetch's cheeks and the cut of his glance was fast hardening into intolerance. "Why pick on me? I'm not the one that's been luggin' in gunslingers – matter of fact I been lettin' men go."

"Yeah. I heard about that. About Mullins an' all them I.O.U.'s. Looks like t' me you got your tail in a crack," Jones remarked, looking the cattleman spang in the eye. "While we're dealin' in facts suppose you tell *me* where you scraped up the money you've bet on this race?"

Rage sprang in Spangler's apoplectic stare and for one stunned moment he stood absolutely speechless, the hamlike fists whitely clenched at his sides. Then he cried in a voice that cracked with wrath, "I don't hev to take that! I don't hev t' take that crap off nobody!"And, roughly shouldering past the shocked faces, the fellow stalked off like a sorefooted bull.

Jones, peering after him, scrubbed a hand across his jaw and then drew a ragged breath, nervously echoed by others. But, unlike these, Jones was not content sheepishly to stare at his boot toes. "Who's he figure 't put on that horse?"

He got mostly shrugs and uneasy glances. But one ranny, bolder or more gabby than the rest, undertook to say: "That Mex'kin, Tavares."

Something jumped inside Jones. "Tavares?"

"Charco, I believe his name is."

"Anyone know where a man could git hold of him?"

Someone else interrupted the tobacco chewer to say, "Last I seen they was headed fer town."

"Thanks," Jones said, and wheeled away.

Probably bound for some bar to pick up an early lunch. The very fact that Trimbo was with the man suggested Spangler was taking no chances on his jock getting plastered or being propositioned.

Since Trimbo's habits were common knowledge, Jones reckoned to find the pair holding down a table at the Aces Up. He

151

considered it also a pretty safe bet the vaquero would be reluctant to do any talking in front of his range boss. Nor could Butterfly see any way to get around this.

It wasn't likely the man could add anything important to what Terrazas had already told him; and when he reached this point in his cogitations Jones was minded to forget the whole thing.

But the basis of any efficient police system was the routine check, so he guessed he'd better get on with it. While a habla with the coroner's cousin probably wouldn't turn up a single new fact, it might at least get a few of the loose ends straightened out.

He slipped off his horse in front of the saloon, but just as he was about to push through the batwings he spied Cathie Grisswell coming down the street behind matched bays in the Gourd & Vine surrey. She saw him too and, smiling brightly, waved.

It was a friendly thing, and doubly so to a man deeply mired in Jones' thankless job. He stepped back into the street and when she pulled up, set an anchoring boot on the nearest hub. "An' how's the wildlife treatin' you, Miz' Cathie?" he asked, unconsciously comparing her with the home-town product.

"Why, that's just what I was about to ask *you!*" she laughed. A woman of the world, she had no trouble assessing the wistful admiration so transparent in his glance. Her own eyes teased, while the world stood still and Jones dredged up the lugubrious grimace of a winded swimmer going down for the final count.

"I don't suppose," she said, "you've seen Mr. Raumeller?"

Jones' expression parched, and beneath the surface he twitched like a fish at first feel of steel. "That golrammed gunny—"

"Oh, Sig's not so bad," she broke in to say defensively – "not when you *understand* him, I mean . . ." and sort of sighed into silence, peering a little uncertain at the look on Jones' face. But Cathie, in the East, had found an answer for everything. Her red lips sprang apart in a dazzling smile, and she reached down to give him an affectionate pat. "Silly! I have a message from Daddy," she explained. "Wouldn't you like to ride along?"

"Some other time," Jones said; then, rather bleakly, "Expect you'll find 'em over on Shed Row."

He touched his hat and stepped back, feeling about as sociable as a centipede with

153

chilblains. How could a woman *be* so taken in as she was?

He went into O'Halleran's and found the Irishman back of the bar. Bellying up, Jones called for a double and took it neat with a toss of the head. Squinting over the glass his stare went past the float of hats, on over the games to find Trimbo hunched at one of the tables with a bottle, two glasses, but no sign of a companion. The feller, of course, might have stepped out back.

While Jones was trying to think what to do, some jasper three shapes to the left of him called: "H'are ya, Tavares! What's that nag gonna do?"

"*Quien sabe, señor . . .?*"

Jones spotted him then, over by the free lunch, a flash of teeth under a chin-strapped hat with a snakeskin band. He had a slight, wiry figure garbed in cow-puncher clothes; and then Jones had hold of him, watching the grin drop off Tavares' face.

Shoving him back a couple of steps the sheriff saw Trimbo coming up with a scowl. Butterfly, waving him off, growled, "Keep out of this, buster!" but Spangler's hardcase kept coming, big hands fisted, eyes hateful.

He came in swinging. Jones used his gun. The barrel caught Trimbo just back of an

154

ear. Spangler's man folded. Jones shoved Tavares toward the green slatted doors.

Outside he said: "All right, let's have it. What's my deputy got against Geetch?"

The man licked dry lips. "He took the ranch of my cousin's father – eet was the firs' place he grab."

"Damn!" Jones muttered, Tavares' disclosure still slapping him in the teeth as he reined away. This certainly opened a whole Pandora's box of disturbing possibilities.

The strongest motive still sat in Geetch's corner, but who could say how long hard thoughts had been hidden and festering in the coroner's mind? It sure must have happened a good piece back, Jones himself having no recollection of it, but a dispossessed heir would not have forgotten. The knife must have turned every time he saw Spangler.

While Jones was still woolling it around through his thoughts, Geetch Spangler, filled with sound and fury and forking the horse he had set out to race, came ramming head-on through the scraggles of traffic. The man's bulging orbs smacked into Butterfly like bullets and, with his horse hauled hard back on its haunches – "Jones!" Spangler yelled in the quavery voice of a gun-shot gopher on his last whistling breath.

The sheriff winced.

The cattleman sat wheezing on his sweat-drenched mount, every eye fastened on him, nobody moving out of his tracks. A woman's strident laughter coming out of the Aces Up tinnily tinkled across the street's sudden hush. Spangler's twisted mouth worked and Jones said reluctantly, "What's chewing you, Geetch?"

"That goddam dude! You know what he's done? Throwed a dam across the Verdigris an' cut off my water!"

Chapter Nineteen

A JAG of wild thoughts stampeded across the windy funnel of Jones' mind. His eyes kind of glazed and then he shook himself like a dog shedding water. "You know this fer sure?"

"Alls I know is one of my men just rode in with—"

"He say the river's plumb dry?"

"Said there's less'n two inches of water comin' through! All summer we been gettin'

156

the better part of—"

"But there *is* water?" Jones cut in.

"About a inch an' a half," Spangler said through his teeth.

"Then I don't see much the law can do about it. Your man see the dam?"

"You're golrammed right! Four miles up river. They had three guys watchin' it with rifles!"

"Well," Jones said, "I'll speak to him—"

"Speak, hell!" Geetch snarled like a rabid wolf. "I'll—"

He broke off, darkly staring, as the sheriff fetched a rummaging hand from his pocket, holding out an open fist to show a pair of discolored-brass cartridge cases. "You recognize these?"

The rancher, motionless, stared. "Shells from a Sharps, ain't they?"

"You know anyone that's got a Sharps they'll fit?"

Geetch, looking suddenly old, tiredly sighed. His eyes peered around and then came back to Jones' face. "Expect you know the answer to that. The only Sharps in this country them shells fit is mine." He turned silent a moment. "You prob'ly won't believe it but I ain't fired that gun in more'n two years."

Jones said, "You mind if I have a look at it?"

"I don't hev the gun no more."

"You know what these shells was fired at?"

Spangler said, "I kin guess."

"Have a try."

"They either killed that printer or Grisswell's mare. But *I* never fired 'em," Spangler doggedly declared.

Jones, after a moment, dropped the shells in his pocket. He didn't say whether he believed the man or not. He swung into the saddle and reined his horse toward the jail.

But, part way there, he found himself suddenly needing a word with Charlie Mullins, and cut over past the stock pens, scowlingly turning something over in his head.

In the stable area he found the crowd considerably large. Jubal Jo had his black head over the stall's Dutch doors, ears cocked as though profoundly taking in the things Hollister Grisswell was telling his trainer. All Jones caught was his didactic tone before the medicine king, discovering him, took the thick cigar from his expressive mouth to smile.

"And how is Price Jones this morning?"

he said easily. "I trust the cares of the shrievalty will not interfere with the display of velocity we're about to witness. I was just remarking to Miss Mullins what a pity it is so many of these people in their clannish distrust of a man from outside—"

"You honestly think," Jones growled, "you're goin' to *win* that race?"

"I consider it self-evident. My dear fellow," Grisswell sighed in his most patronizing fashion, "the chances of Jubal losing are practically non-existent. He has a reach of twenty-six feet, covering that much ground at a single jump." The girl, when he glanced at her for confirmation, nodded. "Spangler, and these yokels that are backing him, are pinning their faith on the notion that a short horse, closer to the ground, will get off on top and achieve full speed in from two or three jumps."

"You don't believe it?"

"I think, in most instances, I would have to agree with the assumption. But," Grisswell smiled. "Jubal – for a hotblood – has a very fast break. Spangler's horse won't gain enough at the outset to overcome the black's greater reach. If you've any spare money jingling around in your pockets I'd advise you to get on him."

159

Jones, after eyeing him carefully, said, "Did you know we'd found that horse Geetch lost?"

"Really?" Grisswell said, barely showing polite interest. "It rather seems to me the whole business of that horse has had no other purpose than deliberately to embarrass me—"

"That why you cut off his water?"

Above pursed lips Grisswell's look became flinty.

"Is there nothing that fellow won't do to gain his ends? Look—" he said irritably, "I haven't cut off his water. Why don't you ride out there and see for yourself? I have simply diverted my own legal share – which I have every right to do."

"It's not like t' make you many friends around here."

"Friends!" Grisswell scoffed. "How naive can you get?" One hand slid into his coat and came out to hold up a fancified red-leather wallet. With a short, snorting bark of a laugh he said, "Here are the only friends *I*'ve encountered."

"That's a pretty hard view."

"It's a pretty hard world." The Gourd & Vine owner put his pocketbook away. "I'm a practical man. I'm willing to recognize

160

facts. The facts of this business are plain. And I intend to protect myself."

Jones said gruffly, "Are you accusin'—"

"I wouldn't waste my breath."

Jones shifted uneasily in the crotch of his saddle. "You've got no proof—"

Grisswell said across the curl of his lip. "You can tell that fellow, anything he tries will be paid back in the same coin with compound interest. He's not dealing this time with poor whites and Mexicans!"

Chapter Twenty

TRIMBO came up and Grisswell, beckoning, took him out of earshot while Jones, plainly fuddled, was trying to pull himself together.

"Maybe, if you'd talk to Geetch," Charlie Mullins began, but Jones shook his head.

"Might's well try t' scratch my neck with my elbow," he muttered disgustedly, and sat a moment scowling, looking at her but obviously not seeing her. "Why'd you quit him?"

"I was tired, I guess . . ." Her voice

trailed away, and then she said, more vigorously, "You asking for the truth or—"

Jones, breaking loose of a look he'd encountered before, hurriedly gathered up his reins, mumbled something unintelligible, kicked his horse into a lope and, slightly red of cheek, departed.

Not until he'd gotten clean away from the stable area did he let his mount ease or draw a truly free breath.

Grisswell had disturbed him – no getting around that. But the look he'd caught in Rockabye's stare was the kind no bachelor was like to tempt more of – no guy, anyway, with all of his buttons. Jones could pretty near hear the squeak of double harness!

It was plain that dude had offered more dough than Spangler had been of any mind to pay her. Feller seemed to think his money could get him just about anything; and it crossed Jones' mind to wonder right then how much of the dude's money was responsible for this star.

It was a sobering thought, not an easy one to live with.

And thinking over a number of other remarks the man had let drop in the course of their acquaintance, Butterfly found himself heading down into Rag Holler, a firetrap of whoppy-jawed tents and ramshackle shanties. It proved no great bother to locate the Potter clan, but getting Potter to unburden himself appeared about as unlikely as anything Jones had yet come up against. The man wasn't looking for trouble and said so.

"I'm not here t' make trouble," declared Jones testily. "Alls I want is a talk with them kids."

"They don't know nothin'."

"Where's that boy you call Dub?"

"What's he done now?" the boy's father whined, bristling.

Jones drew a pair of silver dollars from his pocket, chunking them suggestively from one hand to the other. "That him over there? The one without no shirt?"

Potter sullenly nodded.

"Dub," Jones said, "you kin do the law a favor if you'd say straight out where you toted them notes you got from Mr. Gattison."

The boy, eyes puckered against the sky's livid glare, cocked his head to one side and asked, curling his lip, "What's the law ever done fer the likes of us?"

It appeared to Jones, trying to find a fair answer, that all the hard views were not

163

necessarily held by the moguls of this community. Scrubbing his jaw he shot a grim look at Potter, reconsidered the boy and presently said soberly, "The law's like an old man needin' new spectacles. Means well, I reckon, but t' be of much use he's got t' have the help of fellers whose eyes is still sharp an' clear. There ain't nothin' wrong with *your* eyes, I'll warrant."

The boy, sniffing scornfully, refused to be drawn.

Jones, sighing, took a page from Grisswell's book and held up the silver dollars. "Tell you what I'll do, Dub. I'll swap you these two cartwheels t' have an' spend as you see fit if you'll tell me where you took them notes."

"Took 'em to the Post Office."

Jones, frowning, said, "They was *letters?*"

"Sure had stamps on 'em."

"When you got to the Post Office what'd you do?"

"Pushed 'em through the slot." Dub, advancing, nervously put out a hand and Jones slipped him the coins.

But he wasn't licked yet. There was still Terrazas, and all the way back to town he considered the man they had given him for deputy, and the words of his cousin, the vaquero whose ingenuity or patience had turned up the missing pony. He even dug out the likeness the coroner had drawn of Geetch and stared a grim while at its uncomplimentary aspects.

"Eet was the firs' place he grab," the cowboy, Charco, had said.

With that kind of thing always clawing a man, Jones did not find it too tough to understand why Terrazas could appear so convinced Geetch himself was behind all the things which appeared to be frothing up around them. The man would naturally suspect Geetch; but was that the whole shape of it? Or was Terrazas more deeply committed? Embittered, revengeful, had the man in his brooding hatred of Spangler gone so far as to attempt to steer what was happening?

Certain aspects seemed to suggest he had. There was the night – *last night, actually* – when Jones in his anger had had that run-in with Trimbo. When, disgusted, he had left the Spangler ramrod and Geetch himself at the jailhouse steps to come into the office and find Terraza in the dark with a loaded Greener.

The explanation the deputy had offered, now that Jones was able to take a good look at it, seemed pretty feeble – even kind of unlikely. And there were other things, too, that seemed to click into place as the sheriff traced back through the past several hours a whole series of instances that now appeared a little queer.

Had those letters Dub posted been delivered to Terrazas?

But what was the point in running off with that pony horse? To spur up bad feeling between the two moguls? To drive Geetch into some open attack?

And the gunfighter, Raumeller . . . Had Terrazas been the go-between in securing his services for Grisswell?

The sheriff was plagued by no dearth of questions, but the continuing tramp of his unruly thoughts refused to turn up any very convincing answers. On evidence available Spangler still looked to be the number one choice. The cowman's bullypuss ways had ridden roughshod over too many persons other people remembered and financially at least, the man appeared in bad shape, reduced even to letting a full half of his crew go.

In such circumstances, Jones asked himself, where had the feller laid hands on the money he'd put up with the barkeeps, trying to get well on the outcome of his race? From that Purple Cow holdup? From the pockets of bushwhacked Harley Ferguson?

The sheriff, growling in his throat, morosely pawed at his cheeks as he took in the clabbering jostle of people all bound with their gab in the direction of the track.

He was aware that time was about to run out.

Dreading to see this race come off, he could think of no handle he could pull to stop it. It looked to him to be synonymous with disaster and, unless he could block it, was almost sure to end in gunplay. This was purely hunch, stirred by his conviction the stakes put up had got entirely too high. Geetch's horse, in this go, was a nine-to-one favorite, but if the nag failed to win just about anything could happen – and all of it unpleasant.

If Spangler wasn't behind all the things Jones could sense rushing headlong to a boil, then the stage was surely set by one whose obvious intention was to see the cattleman blamed for it. Question was *who?* Give him the answer to that and the chance to get at the guy, he just might be able to stop this fracas short of a killing . . . but he

167

didn't believe it.

There seemed so many loose ends, so many explosive possibilities. Grisswell with his money and his bitterness toward the town . . . How much of this could be tracked back to him? And Geetch, and that Sharps the cattleman claimed he didn't have anymore. Since *when* hadn't he had it?

A man didn't know whether to believe the old wolf or put him down for a plain-out liar. But Jones, as sheriff, could not afford to stall any longer. He had to take chips. He had to step out on one side or the other, to pick his man and abide by the consequences. And at last, still reluctant, he made up his mind.

Chapter Twenty-One

MOST sprints in the days before starting gates – particularly matched affairs cooked up between owners – took a considerable while to get on the road, and the one in hand at the Tiedown bullring, as the riders interminably jockeyed for position, did little to mollify the buildup of tension.

After a hectic hour spent abortively in scoring, with the sun beating down and the furies of frustration loosening restraint, all the goriest fears at the back of Jones' thought looked scarcely a hand's span from grim realization.

The shouts and catcalls of the crowd grew ugly. No one with money up was minded to leave, and it was increasingly clear they would not tolerate much longer delay. Grisswell's black, fairly trembling with impatience, showed a froth white as soap between satiny cheeks while he fought the bit, sidling, under the girl's tight rein.

The gray Eight Below, Spangler's entry, appeared in somewhat better case but the wiry Charco, perched on his sear singer, seemed like a cornered rat, as his dripping face kept twisting desperate glances across the cant of a protectively hunched shoulder.

What was he scared of?

Afraid Geetch had taken too much out of the horse? Or was he signed up to lose and starting to panic about his chances of getting clear in the event he went through with it?

Jones, thus reminded of Grisswell's attitude, took his own assessment of the possibilities. The crowd – should they suspect they had been sold out – was in no mood either to forgive or forget; and the sheriff, just in case the guy did try to run, was sorely tempted to get back in the saddle, only barely deterred by his notions about Geetch.

Nerved up, distrustful of his own convictions, he remained uncertainly watching, not too far from Spangler who was scowlingly peering toward where the dude stood with his hired gun and buggy boss.

As the riders wheeled back to once again take positions Cathie Grisswell, enticingly garbed in Eastern bridle-path toggery, came up to take Jones' arm with a proprietary smile. "They will surely get away pretty soon, don't you think?"

Jones, without peeling his glance off Geetch, gruffly said he didn't know, and looking somewhat fussed, managed to free his pistol hand despite her attempt to keep hold of it. She said, looking up at him, "What's the matter with you?"

A thud of hoofs brought dust boiling up off the course and Jones, craning his neck, might have been completely alone for all the notice he took of her. Attention jumped to the main event and he could see the two riders bearing down on the score. As they came up to the line Charlie Mullins cried: "Ready?" and Charco Tavares, on the gray shouted, *"Go!"* . . .

Spangler's short horse, under the quirt, crossed the score like something heaved from a catapult, rocketing into a barreling lead that appeared somewhat greater than a full length of daylight. The crowd roared approval and the Mexican, hand-riding, pushed his advantage another half length and he kept that edge for the next twenty jumps. And then Grisswall's black began cutting it down, just as the dude had told Jones he would.

The yells died away. They flashed past the eighth pole, Jubal Jo, driving, scarcely a length behind the gray. And Rockabye Mullins hadn't yet used her bat.

It was sickening the way that big black ate up ground. Every stride seemed to chip away more of the gray's lead. A dozen jumps past the pole brought the thoroughbred's nose almost even with Eight Below's flying tail. And then the black, still driving, began to inch toward his flank. Charco – apparently almost beside himself – was furiously belaboring the gray with his quirt, first one side and then on the other, but the black kept gaining.

"Throw that damn whip away!" Jones could hear Spangler yelling through the crowd's lifted groans but the Mexican, face livid, kept berating his mount as though it was the only prescription for victory he knew.

The black's froth-flecked muzzle now had reached the gray's shoulder and the hard-flogging pound of those racing hoofs had scarcely another fifty yards to go. Every man in that incensed crowd was on his feet, most of them running after the horses toward the finish.

Only Geetch hadn't budged, nor the group about Grisswell whose features had taken on a kind of smug blankness. The Gourd & Vine buggy boss, Eldon Shores, dropped several words from the side of his face which the former purveyor of bottled nostrums seemed to find humorous enough for a laugh.

These were the happy ones. The smart city slickers who had tailored a coup and now could lay back and wax fat on their profits – perhaps even pleased at the plight of this town, wholly indifferent to the havoc they had wrought.

Jones' attention veered back to the track. Now the black's nose showed against the gray's head, both of them pouring their all into this effort, closing the gap between themselves and the wire with ears pinned back and wide, gaping nostrils. The thunder of hoofs beat against Jones' thoughts. So close together were the two horses here it almost seemed as though their riders were crouched knee to knee, cursing or praying or whatever people did when the chips were down and the spoils for the victor only short gasps away. Charco, apparently, had lost his quirt and the gray's stride had lengthened, seeming less choppy as neck and neck they plunged toward that final moment of truth.

It was the girl's arm now that had gone to the whip, expertly reaching back to touch the black just once . . . and then again, more sharply, as she sought in the memory of other times to push that dark nose into the lead. You could see the horse strain – leastwise Jones thought he could, but as they swept round the turn he could still see the edge of one gray nostril beyond the open-jawed muzzle of the black. And that was the way they crossed the finish, with the flag swooping down and the banker through his megaphone crying out the race in favor of Jubal Jo.

Geetch, with his purpling face, looked

crazy – as mule-headedly crazy as a lot of these people had always figured him to be. Yelling, cursing, waving his arms like some bloody mad ape, he went stumbling blindly in the direction of Gretchen as though minded in his outrage to tear the banker limb from limb.

It came over Jones that even a walloper insensible as Geetch might sometimes feel much deeper than you'd think and maybe occasionally – like right here – be able to recognize right from wrong. And one more thing Jones saw, that most of his own notions had fallen short of the truth.

Sure he'd picked his man and in the main been right. Certainly greed and avarice – even, perhaps, some element of revenge, had shown their pinched and parfleche faces. But only indirectly had the core of this squabble leaned toward either range or dollars.

It was sprung from the head, a nasty matter of ego, evolved from twists almost impossible to track down. Driven of course by ambition, but promulgated in a mind that refused to consider accepted truths. This fellow in *his* view was Mr. Big: there was no middle ground that he was willing to stand on. He was a man who had to be first every time, a man wholly ready to kill to make sure of it.

Catching up the reins of the first mount he came to, Price Jones went into the saddle, knowing this bastard had got to be stopped.

The stage was certainly set for murder. In the angry group around the flag-holding banker, Harold Terrazas stood with his Greener like Moses about to destroy the Golden Calf. The twin tubes of that sawed-off iron firm at his hip – having driven back the clamorous mob several paces – were now grimly leveled at the Spangler waistline, and it was plain from his expression the coroner-deputy needed mighty little more encouragement to shoot.

Jones, forcing his borrowed horse into this gathering, bitterly tried to move the crowd some more, a task which met with very little success as resentful losers by the banker's decision furiously cursed his unwanted interference. And over and above all the rest of this uproar the cowman's bull voice like a trumpet from Jericho was bludgeoning the din with the contumelious details of the bank's alleged ancestry.

The man's pasty face showed the pinched

grip of fright as he was jostled and shoved by the hands reaching for him; and Jones, minded to bargain off a little skunk for a bigger one, dropped from the saddle to ram a gun in Geetch's ribs, thus at one stroke considerably diminishing the racket. While the cowman, confused, was twisting his head around, Jones said into the relative quiet: "Git back, you fellers, afore somebody gits hurt!" and, ere the bewildered ranchman could take in what he was up to, he had stepped back himself with a hogleg leveled in each rope-scarred fist.

"Here—" Spangler yelled, "what'd you grab my gun fer?"

Jones, ignoring him, snapped at Terrazas, "Git a rope for our friend the chief commissioner," and saw T. Ed Gretchen begin to shake.

With his penurious eyes almost starting from his head the banker cried: "God, boys – not that!"

An approving chorus of growls from the crowd noisily engulfed whatever desperate appeal the banker in his terror might have made. Some of those faces looked pretty grim indeed until Jones, rather sternly, held up a gun-filled hand.

"How many of you figure that decision

was fair an' right?"

Not a sound came out of that mob of scowling faces.

The vociferous shouts of those wedged round him must have washed out any last hopes the banker had. He almost collapsed. In a quavery croak scarcely louder than a gopher's he perspiringly admitted he might have been mistaken. "It was awful close . . . I guess it could have been a . . ." he said hopefully, "a *tie?*"

Jones could almost pity him, pleading for belief. The look of the man embarrassed him. It was hard to reconcile this Ed Gretchen with the pompous fool of so many self-righteous pronouncements, the Simon Legree of so many hard bargains, the county commissioner so prone to foreclose on any poor slob who couldn't pay up.

But Jones hardened his heart, helped with this by the man's final perfidy which would have made paupers of at least half the town. "Why don't you tell them the truth," he said, "an' confess you knew dang well you was lyin'?"

"I couldn't help it!" he cried. "I had *three thousand—*" and choked, looking aghast at what he'd said.

"Now," Jones growled, "we're gettin'

down t' cases. So you had three thousan' bucks on that race. A pillar of the Church. T. Ed Gretchen, the man who never gambles—"

"But I had no choice! I – You've got to believe me! I was *forced*—"

"I'll buy that if you'll make a clean breast of—"

"What's this?" Grisswell growled, coming up with Shores and a lynx-eyed stare from his fight-for-pay killer.

Jones looked them over. "Bein's you asked I don't mind sayin' your buddy, Ed Gretchen here, has just admitted he mis-called that race. Claimed first off it was your horse won; now it seems he was beat by—"

"What are you trying to pull?" the dude cried.

"*I* ain't tryin' t' pull anythin', mister, an' I don't wanta have t' kill someone over it, but until Gretchen's change of heart gits looked into, the law's goin' t' have to impound all bets. Unless," Jones observed, "you'd be willin' to abide by what your jock says."

"Charlie Mullins?" The dude laughed. Then he took another less-assured look at the man with the pistols. "Why wouldn't I be willing?"

"I don't think she'll lie."

Grisswell's jowls colored up like a gobbler's, and you could see the bluster shaping up in his face. Then, scowling again at Jones' gun, he said testily, "There's no occasion for lies—"

"My sentiments exackly."

The dude, suddenly uneasy, slanched a look at his firepower. "What are you talking about?"

"You," Jones said, "an' a couple of murders. One Harley Ferguson, fer instance, an' a blackmailin' printer. Put the cuffs on him, Terrazas," he barked at his deputy and, swiveling his artillery, brought Sig Raumeller into sharp focus.

Still holding his breath he was beginning to think he might yet bring this off, when everything seemed to come unstuck at once.

Geetch, with a beller that must have reached clean to Tombstone, lunged for the dude like a Green Bay Packer. At precisely this moment Grisswell himself – sold short in Jones' shift to immobilize the greater threat – slammed into the sheriff with a fluttery squawk that swept one pistol completely out of his grasp and flung him staggering into his mount.

The horse's head went down, his hind

legs flew up. The crowd broke apart in forty directions, each guy and his neighbor frantically ducking for cover as Raumeller's guns, jumping into his fists, commenced bucking and banging like an emplacement of howitzers.

Something plucked at Jones' sleeve, something jerked at his boot. Rolling desperately to get clear of those flying hoofs he got off two shots and was trying to get up with no idea of their effect when the deafening double blast of the coroner's shotgun whooshed past his face to knock Raumeller sprawling and drive all lesser sounds into oblivion.

Later, with Grisswell safely locked in a cell, Jones – pouring drinks from the office bottle – sat around with Terrazas and a mellowing Spangler, hashing over the fracas. "Well, I was right after all," the cowman said with authority, "that dang dude *did* make off with my pony horse!"

"Someone from Gourd an' Vine did," Jones nodded. "The idea, of course, was t' git all the mileage they could from your rep while fixin' it t' seem you was out t' bust Grisswell, lookin' fer any excuse you could find. An' them I.O.U.'s you been passin' around sure made it look like you was scrapin' rock bottom."

"I was kinda pinched," the cowman admitted, "tryin' to hold back enough cash to bet on that race."

"What I can't make out," Terrazas said, "is how you got onto that dude in the first place. What made you think it was him that was pushing this?"

"I didn't, straight off. It was buyin' up Spangler's notes on top of the way he had tailored that race, gettin' handbills printed in advance like he done, that finally set me t' diggin' around. Then that hullaballoo about him gittin' shot at with everyone knowin' Geetch had that kinda gun."

"But *why?*" the coroner growled. "The guy had plenty dinero—"

"That's what had me fightin' my hat. It was plain he hadn't no use fer Geetch, then I found out what he thought of this town — hated everything about it an' everyone in it. That didn't seem t' make much sense till it come over me the town had no time fer him either. But everyplace I looked it seemed like Geetch was the focal point, the prime target of all that was happenin'. That's when I realized the guy had a screw loose. He *had* t' be first; he couldn't abide t' stand in someone else's shadder."

Geetch said, "What's his girl goin' to do – anyone hear?"

"Understand she's packin'. Guess she's goin' back East. She's put the ranch up fer sale."

Geetch, swishing the whisky around in his tumbler, had been studying Terrazas in a covert sort of way. Now he said across Jones to him, "If I was t' buy it, would you run the place fer me?"

The sheriff, reckoning this was about as near as the old wolf could come to fiddling around with an olive branch, got up with his bottle and stepped out on the porch, and just in time, as it happened, to observe Charlie Mullins slouching past on her old red roan.

Answering his wave she rode over to the steps. "When you gonna quit poisonin' yourself?"

Jones, scowling, said, "Just as a matter of idle curiosity, which nag you reckon really won that go?"

"Jubal did, by a lip an' two whiskers."

"I hope t' hell," Jones said, "you ain't passin' that around."

Charlie Mullins laughed. "I figure to think about it some. You hear about that hoedown the folks is gettin' up for Saturday a week? If you was to come by an' really put your mind to it, I could prob'ly be persuaded."

MAGNA-THORNDIKE hopes you have enjoyed this Large Print book. All our Large Print titles are designed for easy reading, and all our books are made to last. Other Magna Print or Thorndike Press books are available at your library, through selected bookstores, or directly from the publishers. For more information about current and upcoming titles, please call or mail your name and address to:

MAGNA PRINT BOOKS
Long Preston, Near Skipton,
North Yorkshire,
England BD23 4ND
(07294) 225

or in the USA

THORNDIKE PRESS
P.O. Box 159
Thorndike, Maine 04986
(800) 223-6121
(207) 948-2962
(in Maine and Canada call collect)

There is no obligation, of course.